# DAN TURNER

## HOLLYWOOD DETECTIVE

## NO. 11

# DAN TURNER

## HOLLYWOOD DETECTIVE
## NO. 11

BY

### ROBERT LESLIE BELLEM

"Murder By Proxy", *Spicy Detective Stories*, June 1934; "Crimson Comedy", *Spicy Detective Stories*, December 1941; "Sleeping Dogs", *Dan Turner—Hollywood Detective*, January 1943; "Arrow From Nowhere", *Dan Turner—Hollywood Detective*, February 1943; "Feature Snatch", *Dan Turner—Hollywood Detective*, February 1943; "Shakedown Sham", *Dan Turner—Hollywood Detective*, May 1943; "Fall Guy For Forgery", *Hollywood Detective*, September 1946.

Published June 2021

isbn 978-1-64720-338-2 (trade paperback)

# TABLE OF CONTENTS

| | Page |
|---|---|
| Murder By Proxy | 1 |
| Crimson Comedy | 25 |
| Sleeping Dogs | 69 |
| Arrow From Nowhere | 97 |
| Feature Snatch | 127 |
| Shakedown Sham | 157 |
| Fall Guy For Forgery | 183 |

# MURDER BY PROXY

*"Man killed in star's dressing-room!" the headlines would have read. But this killing never got to the papers!*

Y OU could hear the scream from all the way across the studio lot. It knifed in through the half-open door leading to the dismantled set on Sound Stage "A" like a rusty bayonet through a man's guts. Raw, harsh, nerve-shattering.

I smelled trouble—lots of it. No woman ever screams like that for the sheer pleasure of exercising her throat. In my business—I'm Dan Turner, and I've been a private detective in Hollywood for a long while—I've heard plenty of screaming women. I've heard hysterical screams, screams of anger, drunken yells. But this was different. There was terror in it; sheer, stark, raving fear. A damned nasty sound.

I'd been standing there on the bare sound stage talking to Ed Hendryx, production supervisor for Altamount Pictures. Just a social visit. I saw Hendryx' face go white. He turned and leaped toward the door of the sound stage. I was one jump ahead of him.

Outside, a lot of people were streaming toward the studio's bungalow dressing rooms across the way. One bungalow was larger, more elaborately ostentatious than the others. It belonged to Thesta Milford, Altamount's greatest box-office star. Suddenly the bungalow's door crashed open. A figure came out. A girl. She was running.

From inside the bungalow came another scream. It was louder than the first one. It rasped your eardrums like a saw going through living bones. I yelled at Hendryx. "Grab that girl—the one who ran out!" Then I plunged through the swelling knot of people outside the bungalow door. I hurled myself inside.

Thesta Milford stood in the center of the room. Her mouth was open. She was getting ready to

scream again. She was completely naked.

A LOT of men would have stopped to stare at her. You wouldn't have blamed them much. Her black wavy hair hung down around her bare warm shoulders in midnight ripples. Her firm little breasts stood boldly forth like a pair of luscious pointed melons. The soft sweet curves of her torso melted into flatly-rounded hips and swept on down into the creamy perfection of her thighs and legs. There wasn't a stitch of clothing on her.

But I was looking at her eyes. They were twin black pools of sheer horror, as though she'd just caught a glimpse of some gory hell and couldn't erase the picture.

I grabbed her. I put the flat of my hand over her red mouth. She went suddenly limp in my arms. She fainted.

I supported her dead weight over to a big easy chair and lowered her into it. Then I looked around to see what had caused those screams.

There was a door leading to an adjoining room. It was closed. I opened it. I looked into a sort of combined dressing-room, boudoir and bedroom. Having a bedroom in her studio bungalow was one of Thesta Milford's special privileges. After an especially emotional dra-matic scene before the cameras it was her custom to repair to her studio bungalow, soak in a hot scented bath for an hour, then snatch a nap to recoup her strength. At least that's what the press-agents said.

The boudoir-bedroom was all done in pink—pink-tinted walls, pink-tinted wicker dressing-table and chairs; a pink bed with rumpled pink silk sheets and pillows. Even the low ceiling was pink. And prostrate on the floor was a man. He was flat on his back, and his wide-open glassy eyes were staring horribly up at that pink ceiling. Only he couldn't see it. He couldn't see anything. He was dead.

I recognized him. He was Don Snodgrass, one of Altamount's most promising juveniles. Well, he'd played his last love scene before a movie camera! I knelt down and felt for his pulse. There wasn't any.

I was still kneeling over when Hendryx stumbled in, slammed the front door of the bungalow behind him, and locked it. Hendryx was dragging a girl with him. She was a cute little thing; red-haired and full of fight. She was clawing at Hendryx's wrists, where he was holding her. Her sharp nails were drawing blood. She had on a pert little uniform—a domestic's habit. She was Thesta Milford's maid.

She was panting. The sharp movement of her chest brought her full breasts into sharp outline under the black silk of the uniform. "Let me go! Let me out of here! I don't know anything about this! Do you hear me? Let me go!"

Then Hendryx saw Thesta Milford's nude figure on the chair. He turned the maid loose and ran toward Thesta. He grabbed her by the bare shoulders and shook her. "Thesta! For God's sake, what's happened?"

"She's all right. Just fainted. Throw something over her and come in here," I called to him.

He covered the Milford girl with a negligee. Then he entered the boudoir. When he saw Don

Snodgrass' body he whispered "Christ!" Then he looked at me. "Is he—dead?"

"Very," I answered. I sniffed at Snodgrass' stiffening lips. "Bitter almonds. Poison. Cyanide. This is murder, Hendryx."

"Murder?" he repeated slowly.

I said, "Murder. Better call the police."

Hendryx stared out into the other room. He looked at Thesta Milford. She was still unconscious. He turned and looked at the rumpled pink covers on the boudoir bed. He stared down at Snodgrass' dead body. I knew what Hendryx was thinking. I was thinking the same thing.

I FELT sorry for Hendryx. He was in love with Thesta Milford. He'd have married her long ago, except for one thing. She already had a husband. He was Wallace Dixon, the Western star.

You know how the movies are. Divorces, scandals — they tear down a star's drawing power. Wallace Dixon and Thesta Milford were big shots—the best-known and best-loved couple on the screen. The publicity men had built them up as the screen's happiest married couple. The dear public ate it up. Altamount's contracts with Thesta Milford and Wallace Dixon contained clauses expressly forbidding either of them the privilege of divorce as long as they worked for the company.

But everybody on the inside in Hollywood knew that Thesta and Dixon weren't in love any more. Dixon was running around with some chippy of an extra girl; in fact, he was up Bakersfield way on location at that moment, and he had this dame with him. And it was common gossip that Thesta and Ed

Hendryx were on fire for each other.

That's why I felt sorry for Hendryx. It was fairly obvious that Thesta had been entertaining this sleek Snodgrass ham in her boudoir. A naked woman and a disturbed bed couldn't mean anything else.

I repeated, "Better call the police, Hendryx."

The red-haired maid ran toward the locked front door. "Let me go! Let me out of here!" she shrilled.

Hendryx got a grip on himself. "Shut up, you!" he snarled at her. "Keep quiet and you won't get into any trouble. Open your yawp and I'll throttle you with my two bare hands!" She shrank back from him, suddenly still. Her blue eyes were very wide.

He faced me. "Listen, Turner, we can't call the police yet! The scandal — it'll wreck Thesta's career. We've got to do something. You've got to help, Turner. There's five thousand bucks in it for you if you'll do it."

I saw that he still loved Thesta Milford, regardless of the dead Snodgrass. Then I thought about that five grand he was offering me. Frankly, I'm after all the dough I can get. I've been lucky so far—and I've barged into some pretty tight places in the pursuit of my calling. But some day I'll press my luck too far— if I stay in the game. Then there'll be a nice lead pellet with my name and address on it; and some undertaker will have a job of work to do on me. My ambition is to get my pile and retire before that happens.

Hendryx said, "How about it, Turner?"

I said, "What do you want me to do?"

"Get Thesta out of this. Don't let her name appear. Help me get this body out of here so it can be discovered some place where Thesta won't be involved."

I said, "Okay. Now go outside and tell that mob to beat it. Tell 'em Miss Milford was scrapping with her maid — temperament stuff. Get rid of 'em. I'll try to snap Thesta out of her swoon and see just how much she knows."

THE red-haired maid's blue eyes grew narrow and avaricious. She spoke up grimly. "If there's that much important money floating around, I want my share," she announced. "I want five thousand, too—or I'll spill the whole story! How would you like to see your darling Thesta's neck stretched with a length of hangman's rope?"

Hendryx went pale. "You mean —Thesta—killed him—?"

"You're getting smart."

Hendryx started for her. There was an insane light in his eye. "You lousy—"

I pushed him away. "Beat it—get that mob away from outside like I told you. I'll handle this."

While Hendryx went outdoors to shoo away the crowd, I started on the maid. "Listen, sister. Just how much do you know about this thing?"

"Plenty. I came into the bunga-low a while ago. The boudoir was closed. I—I eavesdropped. Thesta and Snodgrass were in there. I heard him tell her he was through with her. At first she begged him to re-consider. But he said he had another girl; that he didn't love Thesta any more. So she said all right, and would he have a drink with her for old times' sake. He said yes. I heard her get the bottle and two glasses from a drawer. They drank. Then he fell down on the floor and Thesta started screaming. I ran out."

I said, "Okay, sister. Give me your name and ad-dress. I'll be around to see you this evening."

"Bring cash with you," she answered flatly.

"Okay. Five grand."

She said, "And if I want more later I'll ask for it."

I grinned. "That's your busi-ness. Now, get your coat on and go on home and wait for me."

"I'll wait for you, all right," she laughed. Then she gave me her name and address. She was Irene Dobbs and she lived in a cheap apartment off Los Feliz Boulevard.

She went out.

I stepped into the bathroom which opened off the boudoir. The first thing I noticed was that the pink-tiled tub was about half full of perfumed water, and there were a couple of damp towels on the floor. I grabbed one of the towels, doused it under the cold water faucet and took it into the front room. I was slapping it on Thesta Milford's unconscious face when Hendryx came back into the bungalow.

He leaned over her as she stirred and opened her eyes. Her lips parted. She started to scream again. I shoved my palm against her mouth until she got quiet.

I said, "Listen, Miss Milford. I'm Dan Turner, private dick. I'm a friend of Ed Hendryx here. I'm going to try to get you out of this mess. Just keep still."

Hendryx took her hand and patted it. She said, "But Snod-grass—is—is he—?"

I said, "Yeah. He's croaked. But it won't be pinned on you if I can help it."

Her black eyes grew wide with fright. "You—you think I did it?" she gasped.

I kept still. I couldn't think of anything to say.

She turned to Hendryx. "Ed—darling—do you believe I—"

He turned away.

SHE stood up, holding the negligee loosely in front of her. It hardly covered a thing. She had a damned beautiful body. "But—you must believe me!" she cried. "Why—if you think I killed him, then you must think—he and I—were—"

Hendryx took her in his arms. The way he held her against him made me feel sort of funny inside — gave me young ideas. Hendryx said, "Never mind, my sweet." He leaned forward and kissed her lips.

Then his mouth traveled down over her shoulder, like a hungry man's. He kissed the little hollow in her throat. "No matter what happened between you and—and Snodgrass, I—I still love you. Your name won't appear in this nasty business."

She pushed herself clear of him. "Then—you actually think Snodgrass was my—my lover?"

He answered, gently enough, "What else can I think, my dear?"

Her eyes blazed. "Oh, go away from me! I—I never want to see you again! I don't care what happens to me!" She started to cry. She was a good actress. I couldn't blame her much. No woman wants the man who loves her to think she's been going to bed with some other guy.

I said, "Listen, Miss Milford. Get dressed and go home. Hendryx and I have got to get Snodgrass' body out of here so it can be discovered some other place."

She didn't answer me. She went into her boudoir as though Hendryx and I hadn't been there. I liked the cool way she stepped over that dead body there on the floor. No hysterics; no flinching. She started to dress. She drew a pair of thin silk panties up over her smooth thighs. Then she thrust her rounded arms into the ribbon shoulder-straps of a gauze brassiere and adjusted it snugly over her delicious breasts.

I stopped watching her and said, "We'd better

move that body out of the middle of the floor, Hen-dryx."

He nodded. We both stooped over and lifted

Snodgrass onto the bed. Then I said, "What the hell is that?" and pointed.

There was a long, fat envelope on the floor. The body had been lying on it, covering it up.

I picked up the envelope and looked at it. It was addressed in a bold, flowing, heavy handwriting, in green ink. It was addressed to Wallace Dixon at a Bakersfield hotel.

Thesta came toward me. She held out her hand. "Why—that's for my husband! It's the lease to a piece of oil land near Bakersfield. He's up there on location, doing a western picture. He wrote and asked me to send him the lease. He has a chance to sell it for a profit. I gave it to Irene, my maid, this morning to mail for me. She must have forgotten it." She took the envelope. "I—I'll mail it on my way home."

She finished dressing. She went out.

I said, "Now, Hendryx, we'll just cover up the body here on the bed. Then we'll leave it here and lock the bungalow. Tonight we can come back, get it and plant it somewhere else."

He nodded. He was plenty worried. It showed in his face. We covered Snodgrass with a pink sheet. Then we went out of the bungalow and locked the door behind us.

IT WAS already pretty late in the afternoon. I went with Hendryx to the studio cashier. He drew five thousand dollars in cash and handed it to me. "That's for that red-haired bitch," he said. "You'll take it to her?"

I said, "Sure. Tonight. Then I'll meet you and we'll come back here to do something about that body."

I left him.

I went straight to Thesta Mil-ford's home, out in Beverly. A but-ler tried to tell me Miss Milford wasn't in. I pushed past him. Thesta was sitting in the sun room. When she saw me she went ghost-white.

"What—what do you want?" she asked me.

I sat down. I lit a cigarette. "Why did you poison Snodgrass?" I asked her bluntly.

She faced me. "I don't care what you think, Mr. Turner. I didn't poison him."

"Then tell me what did happen."

"I'd just finished a big scene over on Stage 'C.' I was tired. I went to my bungalow. Irene, my maid, wasn't there. I drew a hot bath. I undressed. I got into the water. I must have fallen asleep in the tub. Something wakened me. Like—something heavy falling in the bedroom. I got out of the bath. I dried. Then I walked into the bedroom."

I said, "Go on."

"I—I saw Snodgrass lying there. Irene was stand-ing over him. She looked afraid. She said, 'My God, he's dead!' Then she ran toward the bungalow door. I screamed. Then you came in."

I said, "Thanks. I'll be going." I got up.

On the way toward the front door I noticed a framed picture on the grand piano in the drawing room. It was a picture of Wallace Dixon, the Western star—Thesta's husband. I looked at it. It was inscribed in a bold, flowing handwriting, in green ink.

I went back to the sun room. "Did you mail that envelope to your husband in Bakersfield, Miss Milford?"

She said, "Yes."

"It was a self-addressed enve-lope he sent you, wasn't it?"

"Yes. How did you know?"

The writing was identical to that on Dixon's picture on the piano. But I didn't bother to tell her that.

I went out. I bought a bottle of Scotch.

I got some supper at the Brown Derby. Then I headed for the apartment just off Los Feliz where Irene Dobbs lived.

There was a grinning black boy at the switchboard in the lobby. I slipped him a five spot and showed my badge. "Listen, shine. I want to ask you a question. Do you know Irene Dobbs?"

"Yassuh! She lives in Apartment 16."

"She's Thesta Milford's studio maid, isn't she?"

"Yassuh!"

"She ever have any men friends call on her?"

He grinned a big, wide, white-toothed grin. "Yassuh."

I pulled a newspaper out of my pocket and turned to the theater section. There was an ad for a movie playing at a downtown house. It contained pictures of the several stars who acted in the thing. "Any of these guys ever come to see Miss Dobbs?" I asked.

The boy pointed to one picture. "That gemmun come here lots of times."

I said, "That's all I want to know," and took the automatic elevator up to the third floor.

THE red-haired Irene let me in herself. She was dressed in some sort of black lacy negligee that disclosed a good deal of her body. She had a cute little body, too—all cuddly curves and inviting swells. I took a second look. She didn't seem to mind.

She said, "Did you bring that five grand?"

I grinned. I handed her the wad of bills Hendryx had given me. She counted it and put it in a drawer in one corner of the room. There was a picture on the desk. It matched the picture in the theater ad— the one the hall boy had pointed out. It was a picture of Snodgrass.

Irene closed the drawer where the money was. "That will keep me quiet—for a while."

I said, "How about a little drink?" and hauled out the bottle of Scotch. She got glasses. We had a couple of quick ones apiece.

I said, "I'm warm. Mind if I take off my coat?"

She answered, "Help yourself."

Then we sat down together on a divan and had another drink. I can hold my own with the best of them as far as liquor goes. But after the fourth shot, Irene began to act giddy.

I put an arm around her waist. She didn't protest. I took my other hand and slipped her black negligee down over her shoulders. She had nice rounded breasts, curving flesh. I kissed her. She opened her mouth and darted out her little tongue avidly.

I dropped one hand on the smooth, creamy expanse of her bare thigh. She began to pant a little. I pushed her back on the divan.

She said, "Wait!" in a tiny, excited voice. Then she stood up and shrugged completely out of the negligee. She stood there in front of me. I drank in every detail of her young body. The scanties she wore were practically transparent.

"Am—am I as pretty as Thesta Milford?"

"Prettier!" I said, and grabbed her.

Maybe it was in the line of duty. Maybe I had planned it all in advance. But I liked it, just the same. A man doesn't get opportunities like that every day. What the hell?

She was clinging to me, with her warm arms around my neck. I kissed her some more. She moaned through clenched teeth. "Please—" she whispered.

Suddenly I remembered this was business—not pleasure. All this could wait. I stood up. She pulled the black negligee around her. We had another drink.

I said, "Why did you poison Snodgrass ?"

She took a backward step. "What? Why did *I* poison—"

I said, "Yeah. Why?"

She was just drunk enough to sway a little. "I wouldn't kill him. I loved—"

She stopped. She knew she'd said too much already.

"You liked him plenty, didn't you, baby? He used to visit you up here in your apartment, didn't he?"

"What if he did?" she shot back defiantly.

"Tell the truth. Thesta Milford wasn't entertaining him in the bungalow today, was she? You had him in there. That's why the bed was mussed."

"You didn't know Miss Milford was in the bathroom. She'd fallen asleep in the tub. That's what she told me, and I believe it, because the tub was still full of water when I looked at it. She was so quiet you thought you had the place to yourself. So you brought Snod-grass in for a little party.

She looked plenty scared.

I handed her a drink. She took it. Her hand trembled. She spilled part of the drink down her bare bosom, and gasped.

I looked at her. "Now tell me. Just exactly what happened before Snodgrass fell down dead? I want every little detail. Did you give him a drink?"

She shook her head in a dazed way. "No! I swear I didn't! He was just getting ready to leave. I—I handed him a letter which Miss Milford had given me to mail. I'd forgot to post it. I asked him to drop it in a letter box. He took it —and then he—he—"

"He dropped in his tracks, eh?"

"Yes."

I PUT on my coat and hat "Okay, baby. You needn't worry any more." I went toward the front door of the apartment.

She followed me. "Dan—listen. Why can't the two of us make some money out of this? Nobody knows anything about it except Miss Milford, Hendryx, you and I. Hendryx thinks Thesta did it. She can't prove otherwise. We can make her pay us plenty of blackmail to keep quiet—"

She was clever, all right! She was afraid she might get involved in the thing. She figured that if I joined forces with her in black-mailing Thesta Milford, her own story would never come out. She'd be on the safe side—and she'd make plenty of dough out of the deal, too.

She permitted the negligee to fall open. She stood there flaunting her nice young body at me. "We can have lots of good times together—Dan," she urged. Her breasts trembled provocatively.

I wanted to get away. There was no time for an argument. So I said, "Okay, baby. I'll take you up on it!"

Then I opened the door and walked into the dark hall.

Walked straight into the wicked-looking muzzle of a .38 held in the unwavering fingers of Ed Hendryx!

"Well, double-crosser!" he snarled.

"Well?" I said.

"I come up here looking for you. I figured you'd go with me to get rid of Snodgrass' body. I got to that door just in time to hear you and that red-haired slut planning to blackmail Thesta."

"Yeah?" I said. I was sparring for time. It was a damned nasty spot. Hendryx' eyes were blazing. He looked fully capable of murdering me in my tracks.

"Yeah! But you won't get away with it, see? Because in the first place, Thesta didn't poison Snodgrass. I did. I love her. I was jealous of him. I slipped poison into Thesta's bottle of Scotch in her bungalow. I wanted to kill them both. But I guess Thesta didn't drink her drink. Snodgrass did. Snodgrass died. And now you're going to die, too, Turner! And when I've plugged you, I'm going in to plug that red-headed skirt. Then there won't be anybody involved except me. Thesta will be clear."

I looked at him and said, "You're a liar. You didn't poison Snodgrass." I stared into his eyes. "Thesta wasn't even in the room when Snodgrass died. There wasn't any poisoned booze."

That set him back. In his moment of indecision and sur-prise, I leaped. I knocked his gun hand upward with my left. Then I socked him on the jaw with my right. He went down.

I grabbed him to his feet and dragged him to the elevator. I punched the button. The car came to a stop at the landing. I opened it and shoved Hendryx in. I followed him.

HE WAS still half out when I hustled him across the main floor lobby. I said to the black boy on the switchboard, "Get a taxi. My friend's drunk."

The boy called a cab. It arrived. I pushed Hendryx into the back seat. Then I said to the cabby: "Grand Central Airport, Glendale —as fast as this wreck will get there." I crawled in alongside Hendryx.

He sat up woozily, and felt his jaw. I talked to him—fast.

He listened.

We got to the airport. I found the traffic manager. In thirty minutes he had a chartered plane for me. "Bakersfield," I told the pilot. Hendryx got into the cabin with me. We took off.

We reached the Bakersfield hotel where Wallace Dixon was staying, just about three o'clock in the morning. Hendryx and I sat down in the lobby to wait for daylight.

Hendryx dozed. I was wide awake. I saw the porter bringing in a leather bag full of mail about six-thirty, shortly after the sun came up. I went to the mail clerk. I showed my badge and told him what I wanted.

He went through the mail. He found a thick, oblong envelope. He gave it to me.

It was the envelope containing the oil lease—the one Thesta Milford had mailed from Hollywood to Wallace Dixon.

Hendryx and I took it down to the office of Bakersfield's police chief. He gave it to his chemist.

An hour later we had Wallace Dixon under arrest.

"You see, Dixon," I said, "we know you wanted to be rid of your wife, Thesta Milford. But, because of your contract with Altamount, divorce was impossible. So you decided that there was just one other way. That was to kill Thesta. Then you'd be free.

"You came up here to Bakersfield on location. You wrote Thesta, asking her to send you some papers. You enclosed a return envelope. The gummed flap of that envelope contained enough cyanide to kill three people! You figured she'd lick the envelope and die.

"But she gave the envelope to her maid instead. And the maid gave it to Snodgrass, there in Thesta's bungalow, where Snodgrass and the maid had been having a little party—unaware that Thesta was in the bathroom.

"Snodgrass licked the envelope and died. It was a murder by proxy—Snodgrass died instead of Thesta

Milford."

Wallace Dixon confessed. He was hanged, later, at San Quentin.

# CRIMSON COMEDY

Dan never liked to poke around in other people's business, but this was once when he forgot his good resolutions. He started out to save a man from a beating and found himself involved in a series of the most brutal killings of his career

T HEY wore masks made from handkerchiefs; they were four to one; and they were lambasting hell out of the little fat guy in the baggy tweeds. Nobody likes to watch a good fracas more than I do, but this was different. The odds were all wrong.

I copped an accidental gander at the brawl as I drove past Altamount Alley on my way home from a midnight preview. Even before I ruddered my bucket to the curb I could hear the fat guy's moans, the dull thwack of fists kissing him on the features. The more he pleaded for mercy, the more those four blisters lowered the boom on him.

As a rule, I don't like to poke my smeller in somebody else's personal business. Not without an invitation in the form of cash retainer, anyhow. I've got enough enemies in Hollywood already, the same as any other private hawkshaw. But when I piped the terrific lacing those vermin were dishing out to the corpulent slob, I forgot my good resolutions. Especially when he went down and they began kicking him in the belly.

I cut my ignition, catapulted out of my jalopy and sprinted hellity-larrup toward the center of the festivities. Like a narrow black notch, the alley separated Altamount Studios from the back lot of Super Pix next door. The only light came from a red bulb over an emergency fire exit far to the rear, just beyond where the trouble was taking place. And in the scarlet glow I saw I hadn't arrived any too damned soon.

The fat guy had quit struggling, quit trying to protect himself. He just quivered on the ground, a shapeless blob absorbing copious portions of shoeleather. "Please, boys . . . " he kept whimpering. "I'll pay Shanghai . . . I swear to God.. . "

But the four plug-uglies weren't listening to him. And they were so interested in their football practice that they didn't hear me coming. Which was a break for me. I goosed more speed out of my gams and yodeled: "Belay it, you louse-bound scum!" Then I belted the nearest rodent full in the mush.

I PACK a hundred and ninety pounds of solid heft on my six-feet-plus, and I poured every ounce of it into that roundhouse wallop; felt the satisfying jolt of it traveling up my arm. It was like smacking a ripe canteloupe with an axe. The masked guy's noggin rocked back and a blurt of katchup spewed from his ruined kisser. He folded over, dripping teeth.

His three pals emitted an assortment of startled language, laid off booting the fat bozo and sailed at me. One of them dropped a black-jack out of his sleeve, tried to mace me over the conk with it. He swung like a gate.

I took the blow on my shoulder. It hurt to beat hell. Then it went numb. I growled: "You asked for this, cousin," and buried my left duke south of his equator. Sure it was foul; you don't stop to consider Marquis of Queensbury rules when some sharp apple is trying to cave in your roof with a blunt instrument.

My punch ripped a yowl of agony out of him. He doubled up, holding himself. I pivoted to face the remaining pair. One of them nipped me a lucky poke on the button. Sparks erupted in front of my glims. I gave ground, fought for balance. Another bunch of fives tagged me. I felt my knees go rubbery.

I didn't dare take a count, though. I knew what would happen if I did. Those masked hombres would stomp on me until my kidneys whistled Old Black Joe. So I bought myself a breathing spell by tapping a trickle of claret out of the nearest trumpet. Then I dug for the short-barreled .32 automatic I always tote in a shoulder holster in case of necessity.

The way it turned out, I didn't need the rod after all. Yanking my coat open displayed the private tinware pinned to my vest. The guy with the leaking smeller panted: "Gawd, a copper! Let's get to hell out of here!" Then he and his chum took it on the lam, fast. The last I saw of them they were pelting out of the alley into the street with their hip pockets dipping sand.

The two they had left behind were stretched out cold; needed vulcanizing. But they could wait. The fat slug in the baggy tweeds came first.

He was flopping around on all fours, trying to shove himself upright. I helped him to his wabbly pins, fastened the focus on him. His map was plenty messy in the red glow from the fire exit light, but I

tabbed him in spite of that.

"Lumpy Valanno!" I said.

He tried to answer me; couldn't. He didn't have enough breath available. Not that he needed to tell me anything about himself. I already knew. During recent months he and his partner in slap-stick, Beau Babbitt, had become household words.

ORIGINALLY the team of Babbitt and Valanno had been knockabout comedians in cheap burlesque. Then they had graduated into radio, clicked on the networks with their loony routines. As soon as their Crossley rating skyrocketed high enough, Hollywood had reached out and grabbed them.

First they'd been cast by Superb Pix in a low-budget opus—and the quickie hit the jackpot, coined a fortune. Whereupon Altamount chiseled them away by slipping them a long term starring contract at a staggering stipend. In a sense, it was a raw deal for Superb Pix—but those things happen all the time in the galloping snapshot racket. And now, after cavorting in a couple of lavish Altamount productions, Babbitt and Valanno were on top of the world.

But this didn't explain the assault and bashery just committed on Valanno's pudgy person. As far as I knew, no scandal had ever touched the fat little comic since his advent in Hollywood—no dames, no liquor, no rough stuff. He was just a respectable married guy who'd hit it lucky. Then why the hell had those four masked weasels tried to render him useless?

Remembering something he'd bleated, I thought I might have the answer. I said: "Look, friend. I'm Dan Turner, private snoop. If you need a body-guard, I'm for hire. Rates reasonable, time and a half for night work, no charge for wasted bullets—if any."

He trembled like a cat coughing lollypops. "No . . . oh, my God, it isn't . . . I can't have . . ."

"Okay, skip it," I shrugged. "At least let me see you home and slap a beefsteak on that shiner."

He sagged against the wall. "I can't go home now. I'm working late on some last-minute retakes for our new picture. I just stepped out in the alley for a breath of fresh air when those men jumped at—" All of a sudden he started to wheeze, deep in his gullet. His mitt clawed at his shirt-front.

I've been around long enough to tab cardiac symptoms when I see them. I plunged at him, propped him up. "Heart?"

He nodded, gasped. His lips were turning blue. "Side pocket—coat—quick!"

I dipped my duke in his duds, came out with a fragile glass ampule. I crushed the tiny thing with my fingers, held it under his battered beezer. He sucked in a deep whiff of the sharp medicinal fumes; a touch of color seeped back into his puss. "Thanks," he whispered hoarsely. "But for God's

sake don't tell my wife—she mustn't know the shape I'm in! It would worry her...."

"Sure, sure," I said. "Let's go indoors so you can sit down a while." I steered him to that Altamount fire exit where the red bulb glowed, helped him over the threshold.

Just inside the big sound stage building I gandered a row of dressing rooms. One door had a star on it, with Valanno's name lettered underneath. I popped the portal open, dumped the beefy bozo on a chair—

Whammo! At first I thought we were having another earthquake. Something soft and fragrant and feminine flurried at me, tripped me to the floor, landed on top of me. Raking fingernails stabbed at my lamps and a voice throaty with hysteria yeeped: "You dirty gambler;s thug—I'll kill you if you've hurt him!"

I SQUIRMED under the chiffon-sheathed stems that straddled me. They were long and tapered and nifty to match the tall slenderness of the wren they belonged to. I said: "What the hell!"

She kept digging for my optics. She was a redhaired wildcat in a dress of clingy rayon that adhered to her delishful contours like sprayed emerald lacquer. Where the skirt had hiked northward, you could pipe creamy skin above the garter line, whiter than any she-male thighs I'd looked at in a month of Mondays. Over me, the surging buoyancy of her mounded breasts made my fingertips itch to go exploring; I couldn't help drawing a thump out of the intimate contact of her body on mine, in spite of her efforts to let the juice out of my eyeballs.

Thump or no thump, I couldn't lie there and let her rake her monogram on my map. I rolled sidewise; bucked like a bronco. She lost her scissors hold; went tumbling across the room. I scrambled to her, nailed her with my poundage. "Hold still, baby!" I panted. "Before I slap the bejaspers out of you!"

"You—you stinking *hood!*"

Over on the other side of the room, Valanno oozed his pudgy form up off the chair. "He's not a hood, Sandra. He's Dan Turner, private detective. He just saved my life, out in the alley." Then he told her what had happened, omitting only the heart-attack part of it. He ended up by saying to me: "Sandra is my wife, Mr. Turner."

I turned her loose and we both scrambled upright. She was a vast, lovely blush from her wavy titian hair to the deep-cut dip of her emerald frock. She pulled a shoulder strap back into place and faltered: "Can y-you ever forgive me? It was such a

weird mistake . . . !"

"Not so weird," I said. I fished out a gasper, set fire to it. "Especially when you knew in advance that somebody had threatened to lump him up."

She jerked as if I'd jabbed her with a red hot awl. "I—why, I don't understand what you—" The words died on her gorgeous red kisser as the door opened and somebody ankled into the room.

I tabbed this newcomer right away. He was Beau Babbitt, tall, good looking straight-man in the comedy team of Babbitt and Valanno. He said: "Hey, the cameras are waiting . . . Migahd, Valanno, what happened to your face?"

"I got in a brawl," the fat guy said. "It won't show if I use enough makeup." He dabbed grease paint on his mauled mush, covered it with powder. "Let's go. Sandra, I'll leave you here with Mr. Turner. I think he deserves an explanation." Then the two comedians hauled bunions.

I grinned at the red-haired chick. "You don't have to explain, baby," I said. "I think I'm hep. To begin with, while your hubby was being manhandled, he kept bleating a promise to pay. Shanghai. Then, later, when you hopped me, you called me a gambler's thug. It stacks up to make sense."

"What k-kind of sense, Mr. Turner?"

I said: "The biggest gambling joint in Hollywood right now is Shanghai Mamie's place out on the Sunset Strip. Mamie's got a hard-boiled rep where welchers are concerned. She gets her dough or she takes it out of their hides. The way I figure, your ever-loving spouse dropped a cargo of I.O.U.'s to this Shanghai Mamie at one of her games—and then refused to pay off. So she sent a strongarm squad to teach him a lesson."

SANDRA VALANNO drifted closer to me. Her glims looked scared. "Y-yes, Mr. Turner. You've got it right. Only it was a crooked dice game. That's why we didn't want to pay. And then they began sending threats . . . and we didn't know what to do. Before we could decide, th-this happened." She made a vague gesture in the general direction of the alley.

Which reminded me of the two rats I'd left out there. I said: "Look. I'll toss that pair of vermin in the gow on an assault rap. That'll show Shanghai Mamie she can't—"

"No! Oh, no, Mr. Turner! You *mustn't!*" One jump put the red-haired mama up against me. She twined her arms around my neck and pasted her gorgeous curves to my brisket. "Please!" Then she fed me a sizzling kiss that blistered me to the insteps.

I gasped like a gaffed flounder. I hadn't expected any such ardent maneuver and it startled the curds out of me. I could feel the yielding surge of soft mounds on my chest; the languorous sway of her ripe hips. It was a hell of a swell sensation—but I didn't savvy the reason for it.

I unfastened myself from her leech-like hold and said: "Wait a minute. What cooks, sweet stuff? How come you don't want Shanghai Mamie 's minions in the bastille?"

"Be-because then the newspapers would know about the gambling debt . . . the scandal . . ."

I said: "So what?"

"The t-team of Babbitt and Valanno would be washed up in the movies. At least the Valanno part would." She glued herself to me again; bribed me with her glims and kisser and contours. "It—it would be w-worth a lot to m-me if you'd forget the whole thing—pretend it n-never happened!"

That one maverick shoulder strap took another skid off first base; dropped low enough to show more firm, delicious roundness than was good for my hardened arteries. After all, I'm as human as the next lug—and Sandra Valanno's charms were tempting as hell. I feasted my peepers; couldn't help remembering the thrill I'd got when she had me on the rug a while ago with her legs straddling me. . . .

. . . "Okay, hon," I said. "You win. I won't call copper. But I think we ought to render some patchwork on those guys out in the alley. I left them in bad shape."

She studied me curiously, her lamps shining. "You'd sooner look after them than stay here with me? You aren't going to insist on . . ?"

I said: "Listen, babe. When a wren loves her hubby as much as you do, so much that you'd be willing to pay off that way to keep him out of the grease—well, nuts! You're the sweetest dish I ever kissed but I've still got a shred of ethics. I'll keep my trap zippered about what happened tonight but I won't take a fee for it. Come on. Let's glom a hinge at the alley."

She stood on her tiptoes, gave me a succulent kiss of gratitude. Then the door opened and a voice rumbled: "You filthy son of a witch!"

I WHIRLED; saw Beau Babbitt barging at me with his maulies doubled. "Making love to my partner"s wife—!" he rasped.

Sandra blocked him. "You fool! I was j-just thank-ing him for his promise to keep quiet! He isn't going to tell about Shanghai Mamie, is all. Are you crazy, Beau?"

"Crazy where Lumpy Valanno's concerned, yes. He's my friend. I won't have his wife chiseling on him." His glims scorched her.

I said: "For crysakes, nobody's chiseling. Or would you care for a good stiff swat on the prow?"

When he saw I was leveling, he lost some of his truculence. "Okay. So I was wrong. So I'm sorry." He went to the dresser and picked up his pudgy pal's makeup kit; ankled out.

I looked at the red-haired jenny. "Now that storm's over, how's for a gander at the alley?"

"I'm ready," she said. Her voice didn't even sound ruffled.

We went to the fire exit, opened it, stared outside. The two masked lugs were gone. Either they'd lammed under their own steam or their friends had come back for them. That was jake with me. It took a load off my conscience.

With Sandra hanging onto my arm, I drifted to-ward the brightly lighted set at the other end of the sound stage building where her porky hubby was working with Beau Babbitt in a retake scene. I wanted to let Valanno know everything was serene; all he had to do was send a check out to Shanghai

Mamie's gambling hell and the incident would be washed up. But I never got to tell the little fat guy. He died too soon.

THE SET was dressed to represent an old time wild west bar-room somewhere in Arizona on the Fourth of July. According to the scenario, Lumpy Valanno was a low-comedy tenderfoot from the east while Babbitt played the role of a cowboy addicted to practical jokes. Watching from behind the camera lines, I saw Valanno pretending to doze in a rickety chair near the bar with his brogans resting on the rim of a big brass spittoon. The take was under way and the porky guy was giving out with slapsticks snores for the benefit of the sound track.

An assortment of extras and bit players clustered in the background, going through the motions of swilling skee. Beau Babbitt was offstage, waiting for his cue. Presently the director signaled him.

In the shadowy gloom beyond the Kliegs, a prop man handed a small red cylinder to a jane with hair the color of mellow honey. She was the unit's script clerk—and I twitched a little when I tabbed her. Lisbeth Lennord and I had been on many a party in the old days; she was a cute chick and a hell of a good sport. But the last time I'd met her, she'd been a private secretary in the executive department of Superb Pix next door. It seemed funny for her to be clerking for an Altamount unit now. Quite a come-down, in fact. I'd always figured she was in solid as a rock with the big shots at Superb.

But maybe Babbitt and Valanno had brought her over to Altamount with them when they made the jump, I thought. Maybe they'd got acquainted with her, liked her and talked her into throwing in with them. Or it was possible that Superb had fired her and she'd grabbed the first handy berth. Anyhow, here she was on the Babbitt-Valanno set, trig and smart in white linen skirt and a sweater that would have thrown the Hays office censors into a panic. Just looking at the sweater and its alluring contents panicked my own blood pressure.

She accepted the prop man's little red cylinder, carried it over to Beau Babbitt, gave it to him. He strode onto the set with it; and under the banked lights I saw it was a firecracker. Babbitt went through the pantomime of shushing the extras at the bar. Then he sneaked toward his snoring partner.

I tumbled to the gag. It was a primitive wild west version of the hotfoot. Babbitt slipped the firecracker between Valanno's hoof and the cuspidor; wiped a match on his pants and touched fire to the fuse. He backed off to the far end of the stage, jammed his fingers in his ears, screwed his pan into a grimace.

Alongside me, Sandra Valanno whispered: "Watch this. There's a trick spout under that spittoon. When the firecracker goes off, water will spout up toward Babbitt and those others, drench them. It's a backfire gag, because my husband will go right on snoring—*aeiee-ee-eek!*"

HER scream was a thin thread of sound, almost drowned out by a sharp blast that rattled my eardrums, jarred my tripes. White-hot flames flashed like a miniature sheet before my glims, flame that erupted from the property fire-cracker. Only it wasn't a fire-cracker at all. It must have been loaded with a charge of dynamite.

The explosion was small, vicious, concentrated. I yelled: "What the hell—!" and felt a solid gush of air slamming me off-balance. All around me juicers, cameramen, sound technicians, and assistant directors were scrambling like eggs in an omelette; caterwauling their adenoids out. Dead ahead, the barroom set was a chaotic uproar of overturned props and shouting extras. Lumpy Valanno had been blown off his chair and was flat on his back, not moving. I copped a swivel at his feet and came damned near tossing my cookies. He didn't have any feet. They were mangled, shattered hunks of hamburger.

And now, for a single instant following the blast, there was a silence you could slice like cheese. Everybody was too stunned to say anything. I gulped, got control of my churning elly-bay and went hurtling toward the prone little fat guy; picked up his pudgy left wrist. It was limber in my grasp. I couldn't find a trace of pulse. His kisser was a nasty purple color.

"Get tourniquets!" somebody bleeped. "Bandage his ankles before he bleeds to death! Get a doctor!" Like a wave, people began surging forward.

I straightened up, waved them back. I said: "Tourniquets and doctors won't help. What we need is the homicide squad."

"Homicide—?"

"Yeah. Valanno's deader than fish on Friday. He was bumped."

The defunct guy's red-haired wife—his widow, now—clawed herself through the crush with Beau Babbitt beside her. "No! No!" she wailed. "I don't believe it!"

Babbitt held her. "Steady, Sandra. He's gone. Somebody tried to cripple him by substituting dynamite for my firecracker—and his bad heart couldn't stand the shock." Then the surviving partner stared at a chunky, ape-shouldered prop man on the fringe of the mob.

I looked too; felt my gullet tightening. That prop man was the one who'd first handled the doctored firecracker before it got to Babbitt—but there was something else about him I thought I recognized.

It was his sniffer. Trickles of claret were leaking out of it; the nostrils looked puffy, inflamed. His peepers seemed somehow familiar, too, as if maybe I'd tabbed them above a handkerchief mask not too long ago. All of a sudden I recalled that brawl in the alley; remembered tapping one masked rodent on the trumpet to give myself a breathing spell while reaching for my roscoe.

NOW I said: "Hey, you!" and pointed a finger at him. "When did you get that smack on the smeller?"

He touched it, looked at his palm, saw the wet redness. He stiffened. "Why—why, I g-guess the concussion did it when that thing exploded. My nose bleeds easily—"

I lunged at him. "Like hell. You were one of the four dastards that put the boots to Valanno in the alley a while back!"

He edged off. "What—?"

"Yeah!" I snarled. "You're one of Shanghai Mamie's triggers, bigahd! The one that piped my badge and lammed!" I flicked out my handcuffs, stabbed them at his mitts.

He ducked, swerved, came up with a rung of the chair that Valanno had been sitting on when the blast went off. It was hard and heavy. He balanced it like a baseball bat, swung it, wrapped it around my noggin.

Neon lights pinwheeled through my think-tank. I felt myself falling; couldn't keep the floor from drifting up at me, slugging me on the puss. I took a trip to dreamland.

I WOKE up with the raw taste of rye in my mouth. I hate rye. It's too damned peppery on your tonsils. "Scotch is my tipple," I gargled. Then I pried my fuzzy lamps open, stared up into the beefy lineaments of my friend Dave Donaldson, homicide lieutenant.

Dave's headquarters minions were all over the stage like a herd of termites. Evidently I'd remained under ether for quite a while after their advent, because Lumpy Valanno's remnants had already been carted off to the morgue and most of the extras and bit players dismissed. Now Donaldson pulled his flash away from my kisser and said: "I'll hand it to you, Sherlock. You must have a cast iron skull."

I sat up, touched the sore place. There was a knot on my dome the size of an alarm clock. Over its dull throbbing I could hear a series of feminine whimpers, sobbing, muffled. That was Sandra Valanno on the other side of the stage, mournful as a red-haired Niobe, refusing to be comforted by Beau Babbitt's awkward efforts. She didn't even seem to realize he was trying.

Looking at his strained expression, I could guess how he was feeling. It must have been tough for him to know it was his match that had touched off the jazzed-up firecracker. I couldn't quite decide which one to be sorrier for: the jane because she had lost her hubby or Babbitt because he'd been the instrument of his partner's demise. I wound up by just feeling sorry for myself because my noggin hurt so bad.

I wabbled to my pins, fastened the foggy focus on Donaldson. "Did you nab the guy that maced me?"

"No. The dragnet's out for him, though. I got his name; Pete Hinshaw. They tell me you accused him of being a torpedo for Shanghai Mamie so I sent a squad out to her joint."

That scalded me. Anybody with an ounce of grey matter should know Shanghai Mamie's gambling dive was the last place on earth the ape-shouldered prop man would use for a hideout. It was too damned obvious. If he got any shelter from Mamie, it would be in a much safer place. Her private apartment, for instance. That was in the Gayboy Arms on Wilshire and not many people knew about it.

I was one of the few—and I kept the information to myself. I had a personal score to settle with this Hinshaw louse. I owed him a lump on the crock like the one he'd dealt me; and I was in the right mood to deliver it. Later the cops could have him, but not until I got in my licks first.

So I told Dave Donaldson I felt terrible and wished to drag ankles. He tipped me the nod and I took a powder to my rambling wreck. But instead of heading for home I aimed my radiator toward Wilshire Boulevard and the Gayboy Arms.

It was a short haul. I parked, barged into the lobby, grabbed an automatic elevator and thumbed the penthouse button. Presently I was mauling my knuckles on the door of Shanghai Mamie's lavish private layout.

A YEAR had gone down the hatch since my last visit there, but Mamie still had the same cute little slant-eyed maid—a nifty Asiatic dish with white satin pajamas on her curves and drowsiness in her almond glims. "Why, Mr. Turner!" she said.

"Where's Mamie?"

"I—I'm not sure she—"

"Look," I said. I put my hands on the front of her pajama coat; pushed against softness. "You get Mamie for me or I'll pinch you full of abscesses."

Before she could say anything to that, a voice spoke up from inside. It was a husky voice, like the purr of a tabby-cat. "Let him in, Lotus. Hello, gumshoe. Slumming?"

I drifted over the threshold, sank my tootsies heel deep in plush carpet. The maid lammed and I was all alone with Shanghai Mamie—which is the same as saying I was alone in a cage full of tigers. I broke open a fresh deck of pills, got one going.

"Hiya, Toots," I said through the smoke.

Mamie wasn't what you might have expected of a White Russian jane from the Orient. That description usually makes you picture a stately, regal-looking mama with a hardboiled puss and a shiv in her garter. But Mamie was just the opposite. She was tiny, like a fragile doll. Her hair was drawn back in a sleek midnight bun at the nape of her gorgeous neck; she didn't wear a speck of makeup on her Madonna map. A quilted Chinese robe draped her from throat to ankles, completely hiding her dainty curves. And yet, in spite of that, you knew the curves were there. You sensed them—along with the aura of danger that cloaked her like an invisible warning. She was dynamite.

She smiled at me—and I got goose pimples on my spine as big as jellybeans. Mamie was deadpan except when something annoyed her. That was the only time she ever smiled. She was smiling now. I had a sudden attack of jabber-wockies.

She said: "It's been a long time, Hawkshaw. Have a drink?" She glided to a cellarette, produced a fifth of Vat 69. She had a damned good memory. She knew my preference.

"Thanks, no," I told her. "I'm here on business. I want Pete Hinshaw."

"Hinshaw. Do I know him?"

I said: "Yeah. He's a prop man for Altamount. He's also one of your bully boys. Let's not horse, hon. You're hep to the score. This is murder you're fooling around with now."

She stretched out on a deep-cushioned divan and the quilted robe slid open just enough to show a hint of ivory gams, a peep at perfect little flesh-treasures nestling in a gossamer bandeau. "I don't know what you're talking about," she purred. "Come here. Sit by me. Tell me you're sorry you've neglected me so long."

I perched my heft on the divan's edge; got set to wrap my dukes around her lovely gullet if she tried anything funny. "You aren't kidding me, sweet stuff."

"Stop talking riddles. Be nice to me. Or have you forgotten how?"

"I never forget. I'm just not in the mood, is all. Hinshaw bent a chair rung around my conk a while ago. It drained me."

"Poor Dan." She touched my noggin. Then her arms tangled me and she draw me downward, pulled my mush toward hers. Her kisser was parted, red, moist. The quilted robe gave up the struggle and fluttered all the way open.

I gasped: "Jeest—*hey, damn you to hell!*" But I was too late. She had me. I was locked tight in a jiu-jitsu hold; felt the sharp prickle of a knife-point cutting through the back of my coat to rest against my spine. That was going to cost me a tailor's bill to get the hole sewed up.

Mamie 's glims mocked me. She raised her furry

voice. "Pete. Come here. Bring your boys."

FOOTFALLS sounded behind me. Somebody yanked me off the divan, slammed me against the wall. I blinked and found myself facing four varieties of trouble.

Pete Hinshaw, the ape-shouldered prop man, was one. So I'd been right in thinking I'd find him here. It was small satisfaction, though. The three guys flanking him were the ones from the alley back of Altamount Studios; the rats who'd pasted hell out of Lumpy Valanno. I tabbed two of them from the condition of their pans, the marks of my own dukes. Now, evidently, it was going to be their turn.

Hinshaw rubbed his inflamed smeller. "Hello, snoop."

"Hello, killer."

He scowled. "Don't call me that, wise guy. You did it once on the sound stage. You know what it bought you."

Shanghai Mamie glided forward. "You're an awful dope, Dan. First you butted into something that was none of your business—a little matter of teaching Valanno he shouldn't welch on his bets. And then later, when he happened to get chilled, you tried to pin it on an innocent man."

"So Hinshaw's innocent," I said. "Who told you?"

"He did. I believe him. Apparently you disagree. That's too bad, Dan. It's going to cost you a lot of trouble." She turned to Hinshaw and his buddies. "All right, boys. Let him have it. Keep remembering all he's done to you—and don't pull your punches." Her dark peepers were glowing and she raised her hands to her tiny breasts; pressed them flat as if to quiet the pulsations that made them surge against the brassiere.

I said: "You brazen little sadist!" and made a lunge at her. She side-stepped; and then a fist bounced off my whiskers, damned near caved in my bowsprit. That made another debt I owed to Pete Hinshaw.

But this was no time to think about paying it. I knew I was in for a larruping if I stayed on my feet. So I walled back my optics, let my gams sag. I hit the rug. I didn't move.

I heard Mamie saying: "You idiot. I wanted him mussed up, not cold-corked. No use kicking him. He wouldn't feel it. Get out."

"Out—?" That was Hinshaw sounding startled.

"Yes, out. For all we know, the cops may be following this bright boy. You mustn't be found here, any of you."

Hinshaw said: "So what if they do find us? I keep telling you I don't know anything about that dynamite firecracker. If there was a switch in my props, it happened while my back was turned. . . . Cripes! Wait a minute! I just thought of something!"

"You haven't got what it takes to think," Shanghai Mamie's voice sounded vicious with disappointment. My quick fold-up had frustrated her out of a cargo of thrills. "What is it you think you're thinking?"

"That honey-haired wren," Hinshaw said. "That script clerk. The one with the sweater full of oomph. Lisbeth Lennord, her name is."

"Well?"

"*She* could have switched that firecracker. I gave it to her first, then she passed it to Babbitt. Maybe she handed him a different one."

"Why?"

"Well, look. She used to be in thick with the biggies over at Superb. You know, where Babbitt and Valanno were before Altamount chiseled them away."

"And—?"

"Suppose those guys over at Superb were sore at losing their comedy gold mine. Suppose they planted this Lennord bim with Altamount for a revenge stunt? Like maybe crippling Valanno—so the team would be busted up. Only they didn't know the fat slob had a bum ticker, any more than we knew it when we belted him around."

"I think you're nuts," Mamie said. I wanted to shout agreement but I didn't dare. If I let them know I was conscious, they'd kick the bejoseph out of me. All the same, I knew this Pete Hinshaw was just trying to rig a fall guy so he'd be out from under the murder rap himself. Only when he picked Lisbeth

Lennord he was watering the wrong stump. I knew her too damned well to consider her as a suspect.

Hinshaw growled: "Okay, so I'm nuts. But suppose I drop in to see this Lennord jessie? Suppose I happen to find some left-over dynamite in her stash?"

"By planting it there?" Shanghai Mamie said.

"Hell. Maybe I wouldn't have to. Maybe I could twist a confession outa her."

MAMIE'S voice perked up.

"That would be nice. You could bring her here so I'd be able to watch. I think I'd like that." Her tone droped to a purr again. "But first there's another job."

"Yeah? What?"

"Go see Beau Babbitt and Mrs. Valanno. Tell them we want our money."

"But it was Valanno that owed us—"

"He is dead. They are alive. As far as I'm concerned, they're responsible for the debt. If necessary, we'll use . . . persuasion."

"Listen, Mamie. You know I'm red hot right now on account of Valanno getting chilled. I can't—"

"On your way. All of you. Get that money. Then see about this Lennord girl. Handle her properly and you won't be red hot with the cops. Move, now!"

I heard them pad-padding across the rug's deep piling; then a door opened, closed again. I took a chance, opened my windows, gave forth with a hollow groan. I also bit a chunk out of the inside of my cheek so a worm of crimson would streak down over my chin. Shanghai Mamie was goofy over gore.

She came to me; dropped to her knees. I could smell the perfume of her hair, the warmth of her body. She was breathing fast. "Dan, honey . . ."

I said: "Aw, *nuts!*" made a loose fist and clipped her on the button. A dribble of froth came out of her mouth, like steam. She relaxed.

I jumped up, shivered and got the hell out of there.

MY HEAP can wind up eighty in an emergency. I souped it to ninety, going out Wilshire. Pete Hinshaw and his three henchmen had a ten-minute start on me already. If they got to Sandra Valanno and did anything dirty to her, I promised myself I'd take them apart inch by inch, strew them all over the precinct. I liked that red-haired wren; liked the memory of the pash-bribe she'd tried to give me in her hubby's dressing room to save him from scandal. Now that Valanno was deceased, she needed somebody to look after her. And I was the guy for the job.

There was another cutie involved: Lisbeth Lennord, the honey-haired script clerk with the sweater full of lure. I liked her, too. But she was second on Hinshaw's list of calls to be made tonight. She could wait. After all, I'm not twins.

The Valanno tepee was a fairly modest Spanish-modern layout just this side of Beverly. I made it without turning up any motorcycle bulls, which was a miracle at the speed I was going. Every time I rounded a corner my tires sang soprano.

Pretty soon I tossed out my anchors, skidded to a shuddering stop. I slapped my brogans up a flight of terraced steps, gained the tiled front patio, leaned on the bell push.

Lights came on in the entrance hall. The door opened. Lumpy Valanno's widow stared at me. "Mr. Turner—!"

I said: "Thank God you're okay, kiddo."

Then I spotted Beau Babbitt standing behind the curvesome red-haired cupcake.

He scowled at me. "What made you think she might not be okay?" he wanted to know.

"Because a detachment of Shanghai Mamie's thugs are on their way here with malice afore-thought," I said. "Mamie wants her dough. The geetus Valanno should have paid her."

Babbitt rubbed his cheek. It was fiery red; you could see the clear outlines of fingerprints against his shave. "Shanghai Mamie's men have already been here. They're gone."

I said: "What?"

"Y-yes, Mr. Turner," Sandra said dully. "They m-made threats. So we p-promised to send them the money."

"*I* promised," Babbitt corrected her gently. "I have enough annuities laid aside to take care of us the rest of our lives, even though I never make another picture." He started to slide an arm around the red-haired babe's slender waist, then seemed to reconsider it. I guess he just remembered her hubby was fresh dead.

I peered at the fingermarks on his puss. "You get slugged a little, friend?"

"One of them hit me in the face, yes."

I said: "They play rough," and turned to Sandra; smiled into her tense expression. "Where's a phone? I've got to call the gendarmes."

She pointed. I picked the hand-set out of its cradle, dialed headquarters. I asked for homicide, got Dave Donaldson. I said: "Turner talking. Listen fast. I was right about that prop man being on Shanghai Mamie's payroll."

"Pete Hinshaw, you mean?"

"Yeah, Hinshaw. He and three sluggers are on their way right now to pull a snatch. A jenny named Lisbeth Lennord is their meat. She—"

"I know her. Script clerk on that Babbitt-Valanno unit. I interviewed her on the set, turned her loose."

I said: "For the love of What's-His-Name, will you quit interrupting me? Here's the lowdown. Lisbeth Lennord used to work for Superb Pix. Superb is the studio that lost Babbitt and Valanno to Altomount.

Lisbeth is one of the people who handled that doctored firecracker tonight. So now this Pete Hinshaw
is going to put the snatch on her, try to bop a confession out of her—make her admit Superb bribed
her to plant the explosive."

"So that's it!" Dave roared. "I never thought of
that angle! You think Hinshaw's right, Philo?"

I said: "How the hell should I know? The point is,
you can round up the whole damned works if you
move fast. Otherwise the Lennord gal is liable to get
her profile bashed. Know where she lives? Good.
Meet me there—and get the lead out of your frame."
I rang off, made for Sandra Valanno 's front door.

Beau Babbitt blocked me. He looked grimmer
than a carload of caskets. "I couldn't help hearing
what you said, Turner. And I'm going with you. If
that Lennord witch killed my partner, I'm going to
be on deck when she's nailed to the cross."

"Me too," Sandra said quietly.

I told them that was okay with me. We bounced
out to my bucket, piled in. I kicked my cylinders to
life, stoked them up past the safety zone. We went
away from there in a shower of dust.

LISBETH LENNORD lived alone in a self-effacing
bungalow near Yucca and Argyle. I blistered the as-
phalt, cut a screeching hole in the night. By the time
we got to our destination my jalopy was bleeding
steam from every pore.

When I parked I noticed another heap already at the curb, a black sedan that somehow reminded me of an undertaker's hearse although it didn't actually look like one except in my imagination. I guess it was my knowledge of the honey-haired script clerk's jeopardy that gave me the impression. Anyhow I knew Pete Hinshaw and his pals were on the job, and got to the Lennord frill's stash ahead of me. It wasn't just a hunch, either. I could hear a faint she-male yeep from inside. It spelled trouble.

I slung myself to the pavement, raced for the porch. Beau Babbitt was on my heels but I said: "Get back. Take care of Sandra. There may be shooting—and these lads don't carry cap pistols." Then I hit Lisbeth Lennord's front portal with my hurtling beef.

It splintered inward. I yanked out my heater, thumbed off the safety catch. Then I went blamming into the living room. I rasped: "Lay off before I start spraying poison out of this Flit gun."

THE tableau in front of me was something to remember. Hinshaw, the ape-shouldered property man, had the Lennord quail up against a wall. He was backed by his three burly bullies—not that he needed them for what he was doing to the chick with the ripe honey hair. Hinshaw was the kind that could cop the duke over a woman any day in the week.

He had ripped Lisbeth's sweater open from neck to Nebraska, likewise snagging her brassiere in the process. Now that fragile embellishment hung in peek-a-boo tatters over skin that was like peaches and cream. There were bruises marring her snowy shoulders; her glims were deep azure pools of fear. Her unpent coiffure streamed like a golden waterfall around her white throat and down on her throbbing charms—and the vision of velvety epidermis peeping through a mist of yellow tresses thrilled me to the shoestrings.

But the bruises made me see eleven shades of red. I tapped a tattoo on Hinshaw's spine with my lift mitt, kept his three chums covered with the rod in my right. "Turn, bud," I said.

He let go of the wren, spun to face me. I corked him square on the sore nostrils with a left hook. Twin streams of gravy made a mess of his necktie. "Damn you to hell—!" he whined.

I said: "That's just interest on the debt I owe you, cousin. The worst is yet to come."

"You can't—"

I popped him again, just to show him how wrong he was. When his pals stirred I waved my gat at them. "Freeze, all of you. Unless you hanker to have yourselves air conditioned."

Hinshaw's cheeks twitched. "Listen. snooper. Let's talk this over."

"Talk won't help," I said. I flicked a glance at Lisbeth Lennord. "Go sit down, babe. Tell me how far these illegitimates went with you before I arrived."

She sank into a chair, tried to pull the sweater shut over her delishful breasts where they swelled ripely out of the torn place. "They j-just hit me, is all. And Hinshaw ripped m-my clothes. . . ."

"Nothing else?"

She blushed. "N-no. Except he—he accused me of switching that property firecracker for one with a charge of high explosive in it."

"Guilty or innocent, hon?"

"Innocent, of course! I wouldn't —"

FROM behind me a flat voice said:

"*Somebody* did it. *Somebody* gave Beau Babbitt the one that killed my husband." That was Sandra Valanno coming into the room. She had Babbitt with her. I suppose they'd got tired of waiting out in my coupe.

Pete Hinshaw copped a hinge at the hatred that glittered in the red-haired widow's peepers. "It wasn't me, lady!" he whined. "Honest to God it wasn't. Yeah, I admit me and the boys gave your old man a pasting. But that was something else. We didn't have a damned thing to do with that firecracker switch."

"You say," Beau Babbitt growled.

"I say. And I'm leveling. Why the hell do you think we came here to see this Lennord bim?"

"To frame her," I lifted a lip.

"Ix-nay, shamus. To make her yodel the truth. She handled the firecracker after I did. *She* gave it to Babbitt. Why, the filthy little slut's guilty as hell!"

I whopped him across the mouth. "Watch your language, punk. And if you've got any accusations to make, wait until the bulls get here. Make it official."

"Here—the bulls? God!" he cringed.

Beau Babbitt rasped: "Look, Turner. We're wasting a lot of time. Why don't you search the house, see if you find anything that might incriminate Miss Lennord?"

"You make the frisk." I said. "I'm busy keeping these guys covered."

Babbitt began like an amateur. Lisbeth Lennord crouched dully in a chair; watched him with apathetic lamps. Presently she choked: "Wh-what do you expect to find?"

He picked up her pocketbook from a corner table, got it open, looked inside. Then his map contorted. He breathed: "By heaven, *this* is what I expected to find!" And he held up a small crimson cylinder. A firecracker.

For a split second everybody got so quiet you could hear a change in the climate. Then hell boiled over. Pete Hinshaw bellowed: "That's it! That's the original prop! Now I see what happened! I gave it to this Lennord broad and she switched it, put it in her purse, handed Babbitt a phoney charged with dynamite! Come on, boys—let's blow!"

And he splashed himself at the door with his three pals trailing him like tails to a comet.

I'd been so interested in the firecracker that the move almost caught me with my rompers at half mast. But not quite. I've got quick reflexes. I barreled across the room, body-blocked the prop man, fetched him a jolt on the haircut with the muzzle end of my cannon. That bashed him into his buddies and they all went down like a tangle of pretzels. One of them managed to pull his roscovitch. He aimed it at me.

From the doorway, Dave Donaldson's voice rumbled like thunder with sandpaper on it. "Target practice. Just what I've been needing." A service .38 yammered: "Ka-*chow!*" and the guy on the floor dropped his heater, fixed the stupid focus on his shattered wrist.

Then Dave and a handful of homicide heroes lumbered into the room.

I said: "Thanks, girls. You're just in time."

DONALDSON beetled his brows.

"In time for what?"

"The blowoff," I said. "This cleans up the Valanno kill."

Pete Hinshaw pushed himself off the rug. "You can't pin that on me! I'm just a prop man—"

"But you carry Shanghai Mamie's sideline," I told him. "Criminal assaults wrapped up to take home."

"That's not murder! I—"

I said: "Skip it." Then I looked at Lisbeth Lennord. "About that firecracker in your bag, hon."

"Dan . . . my God, please . . . you don't really believe I did that, surely. . .?" She trembled toward me, forgot to hold that torn sweater together. Her creamy, mounded breasts heaved up and down with her gasped breathing. Her puss was as pale as milk from an anemic cow.

I had a hell of an impulse to grab her, maul her quiet—but I don't always obey my impulses. I said: "Back off and pipe down, sis. I'll do the talking now."

Dave Donaldson grumbled: "Then do it. Before I blow my topper."

"Okay," I said. "Lumpy Valanno 's croaking was premeditated—by somebody who knew he had a faulty pump. Understand, the doctored firecracker wasn't loaded heavily enough to blow Valanno dead. That would have endangered everybody else on the set. But it carried just enough of a charge to shock the little fat guy's ticker out of action."

Donaldson gave me the fishy glimpse. "Come on, Sherlock. Pali your rabbit out of the hat."

I gave myself a gasper, set it afire. I said: "A short while ago I went over to the Altamount lot." This was a lie, but I had a damned good reason for it. "I had them run me a rush projection of the scene where Valanno was cooled. Just as I expected, the camera caught somebody in the act of turning away from the blast, ducking before it went off."

Sandra Valanno grabbed my arm. Her pinkies sank into me so hard I could hear my marrow squishing. She said: "But that—that would mean—"

"Yeah. This party knew what force to expect out of the explosion. And it was the same guy who planted the real firecracker in Lisbeth Lennord's purse just now—the original firecracker which he'd had in his pocket ever since he switched it for the doctored duplicate, back on the set. We'll prove that scientifically by microscope examination of the dust from his pocket. His will be the only duds to show gunpowder dust—hey, Dave! There he goes! *Nab Beau Babbitt!*"

THE tall and handsome straight man in the late lamented comedy team of Babbitt and Valanno was already on his way to the nearest window. When I yelped, he wheeled. He had a gun in his mitt. He cut loose with it.

I cut loose with mine first; splintered his right kneecap. His chattering rod hosed slugs all over the room as he went down in a cursing heap.

Donaldson lunged at him, kicked the gun away. "That'll cost you, brother."

"You—damn you—you'll never prove—"

I said: "Maybe I couldn't have proved anything. But I ran a hell of a good bluff—and you gave yourself away. *Dead* away, if you consider the gas chamber where you'll wind up," I added.

"You can't send me to the gas chamber for trying to shoot my way . . . out of a . . . lousy . . . frameup. . . !

"Not if your bullets had gone wild. But glom a gander. You just croaked two of Shanghai Mamie 's hoods—including her pet crippler, Pete Hinshaw."

"God . . . oh, my God. . . ."

I said: "Your scheme to brown Lumpy Valanno was plenty nifty. You figured nobody would suspect you of bumping your partner. In fact, people would be sorry for you because you'd been slipped a dynamite cracker causing his decease. That was nice thinking. But I began to get hep when I remembered a few things."

"Such . . . as . . .?

"Your jealousy when you caught Valanno's wife dishing me a little kiss. That didn't register with me at first; but it jostled my think-tank later. When I called at Sandra's wikiup a while ago, you had red fingermarks on your mush. You said Shanghai Mamie's boys had bopped you. I know you were lying. Shanghai Mamie's hired hands never slap. They punch—with their fists."

"W-well. . .?"

"You had been slapped, hard. Nobody was with you except Sandra herself. So I doped it out that you must have made a pass at her and got a stinger across the map."

The red-haired widow said: "You—you're right,

Mr. Turner. He did try to m-make love to we!"

"So there was the motive," I concluded. I blew smoke in Babbitt's twisted kisser. "You were in love with your partner's wife. You wanted her so damned badly you were willing to cool him, put him out of the way for keeps. You admitted as much when you said you had enough annuity geetus stashed away to take care of Sandra and yourself even if you never made another pic. That proved you were hoping to marry her when things died down.

"So I set a little trap for you. I let you overhear my phone conversation with Lieutenant Donaldson concerning the possibility of Lisbeth Lennord's guilt. I knew you'd insist on coming here to her joint with me. I figured you'd try to plant the firecracker on her. And now your cook is goosed."

He stared past me; glued his glassy gaze on the voluptuous red-haired Valanno widow. "I did it . . . for you . . . I was crazy over you . . . I had to. . . ."

Sandra Valanno cleared her throat. She dredged up a chunk of phlegm. She spat it in his face.

Then she turned around and walked out.

AFTER the prisoners and cops and corpses were gone, I found myself alone with Lisbeth Lennord. She said: "Dan . . . oh-h-h, Dan, how can I ever thank you enough? How can I p-pay you?"

I ran my fingers through her mellow-honey colored hair. It felt soft, silky; smelled nice. "I've got special fees for script clerks, kiddo," I said.

# SLEEPING DOGS

Dan Turner was interested in good green folding lettuce, but once in a while a case turned d up which made the issue at stake worth more than the geetus in. volved. This was one of them

HE WAS a handsome son of a gun, I'll say that much for him. But the minute he came ankling into my office I knew he was worried about something. That's my business: putting a stop to other people's worries. And that's why plenty of citizens here in Hollywood are personally acquainted with the sign on my door that reads *Dan Turner, Private Detective.*

Anyhow, there stood Geoffrey Jackman looking upset. He was almost as tall as I am—six feet plus—and except for the scars on one side of his map and the black patch where his right glim used to be, he still looked pretty much like a movie hero. A property bomb had prematurely exploded on the set one day, wrecking his mush and his acting career simultaneously. Since then, though, he'd attained new fame as a director.

I opened the lower drawer of my desk, hauled forth two glasses and a fifth of Vat 69. "Have a snifter and tell me what's nibbling on you," I invited.

He poured himself a copious slug, downed it neat. It didn't seem to take the edge off his jitters,

however. His one good peeper had an uneasy gleam and he kept licking his scarred kisser as if he didn't like the taste of the words he wanted to spill.

I kept quiet. Letting the other guy do the warbling is one of my stocks in trade. And presently Jackman decided to unbutton his lip.

"It's about Leneta Leonard," he said.

I wasn't particularly surprised. The Leonard quail was Galatea to Jack-man's Pygmalion. She'd been an

obscure and mediocre extra wren when he took her in hand; and he'd made a star of her—a big one. Her box office pull equaled anybody's in Hollywood, and Jackman's directing was responsible.

He helped himself to another shot of Highland tonic. "Leneta's in a jam. A bad jam. She wants your help."

I said: "Why didn't she come up and tell me about it personally?"

"She's afraid to. She doesn't want anybody to know she's calling you in on the deal."

"Somebody already knows," I said casually.

He stiffened. "Wh-what—?"

I reached into my pocket, pulled out an envelope, handed it to him. He opened it and three nice crisp thousand dollar bills fluttered forth. Jackman's breath made a wheezing, startled noise in his gullet as he read the note that had accompanied the geetus.

I knew what it said, by heart. It had been shoved under my door that morning, hand delivered; no stamp, no postmark to trace its origin:

*"Dan Turner*

*It will be healthier for you if you lay off any case Leneta Leonard might ask you to handle. Here's three grand for being smart. Try a double cross and you'll wake up shaking hands with the angels.*

*—A friend."*

Jackman gave me back the note. "Well, that out-bids me," he muttered sourly.

"Meaning what?"

"Leneta's almost broke and so am I. Bad investments."

To me, this remark sounded like the old malarkey. He dragged down plenty of lettuce as a Paratone director; and the Leonard cupcake's weekly take was even fatter. I couldn't see how they could both be busted, this side of buying the Golden Gate Bridge from some confidence expert.

All the same, Jackman stuck to his story. "Between us, Leneta and I couldn't rake up more than five hundred apiece," he made a bitter mouth. "And besides, your effectiveness would be reduced by this person's knowledge that you're on the case." He gestured toward the anonymous letter.

That scalded my tripes. Frankly, I'm out after the heavy sugar. Luck can't be with me forever; and some day there's going to be a lead slug all tagged with my name and telephone number. I crave to get my stack of chips and quit before the law of averages lays for me with a bellyful of bullets.

So under ordinary circumstances I'd have glommed onto the three grand in the envelope; told Jackman to take himself and Leneta Leonard's troubles elsewhere. But when he pulled this crack about my effectiveness being reduced, he made me bullheaded.

I REACHED for my phone, dialed the *Examiner's* want-ad department. "Take a personal ad," I said. Then I dictated it. "Friend. Send a messenger for your three G's. I'm running my own business to suit myself. Dan Turner."

Geoffrey Jackman hung the curious focus on me as I rang off. "Did you really mean that?"

I said: "Yeah. Now gargle your grief on my shoulder. You've just hired yourself a private snoop."

He hesitated. "Thanks. But look. In the first place, I don't want you to get me wrong. Leneta and I are just good friends—nothing more."

I let this slide. For all I knew, Jackman was leveling. Rumor had never linked him with the Leonard cutie.

So I nodded, kept my yap zippered.

"Leneta's in love with Victor Croft." Jackman stated it flatly, as if he were telling me something I didn't already know. As a matter of fact, I'd heard it from various sources. Victor Croft was a newcomer in the galloping snap-shots; a tall, dark bozo with a

smoothness that knocked the she-male customers in the aisles every time he pranced across the screen.

"So Leneta's in love with Croft," I said. "So what?"

"They're to be married next month. I'm in favor of it. I want her to be happy. But . . . she's being blackmailed. That's why she's broke. She's already paid out a hundred thousand dollars. Half of it was money I loaned her. And she's being bled for more."

I fished out a gasper, set fire to it, let the smoke cover my astonishment. I couldn't quite bring myself to imagine the Leonard lovely as the victim of a shake-down. In my game it pays to keep an ear to the ground for gossip, and I hadn't heard a single whisper of scandal in connection with her.

"What's the blackmail based on?" I asked.

Jackman's one optic got shifty with embarrassment. "She made a mistake when she came to Hollywood three years ago. She—well, she fell into the hands of a producer who made shorts of the burley-cue type. She appeared in one of his reels. Nothing terrible about that, of course, but it'd be embarrassing to have it turn up now that she's a star."

I nodded, poured him another drink.

HE tossed it off. "After she'd made it, I happened to meet her and see possibilities in her. I was willing to gamble on her future."

"It was a fair gamble," I said. "You hit the jackpot."

He nodded. "That's true. It's also true that I went

to the creep who had produced the burleycue reel; bought it from him to protect Leneta. I destroyed the negative and, as I thought, all prints—"

"I can guess the rest," I said.

"One print escaped you. It's still in existence; and now it has turned up. Whoever has it is threatening to make it public, eh?"

Jackman rasped: "Not public, exactly. Something just as bad, though. The blackmailer threatens to show it to Victor Croft. If that happens, Croft would ditch her—and she loves the guy. She'd go to pieces if he broke the engagement. That's why she's paid so much money to get the film—but this shakedown artist hasn't delivered."

"So you want me to locate the film, destroy it," I said.

"Yes."

"That ought to be easy. Who's the louse that made the opus in the first place?"

Jackman's kisser twisted grimly. "He's dead. His organization is scattered. There's no angle in that direction."

"Then I'll find another direction," I stood up. "Leave it to me. And quit jittering."

He gave me a crooked smile and a handshake; scrammed. As soon as he was gone I picked up my phone, called a friend of mine who works for the clearing house association; a mug that owed me some favors.

When I made connections I said: "Turner talking. I want you to trace three thousand dollar bills for me." And I gave him the serial numbers of the dough that had been enclosed with the anonymous letter that morning.

"Okay, Sherlock. I'll call you back."

I waited. In an hour I had the dope I wanted. The three G-notes had come from the Hollywood-Tenth National Bank; part of a ten grand withdrawal from Leneta Leonard's own account. She'd cashed the check herself just a week ago.

"Much obliged, pal," I said, and hung up. Then I barged down to my parked jalopy; headed for the Leonard cookie's wigwam in Beverly Hills. There were some things I craved to know.

In the first place I wanted to find out if Leneta's engagement to Victor Croft was on the level. A lot of that stuff is strictly out of some publicity agent's dream book; and if this particular love affair turned out to be phony, the case would be tougher than boarding house steak.

On the other hand, if it proved to be straight goods I figured I had a possible motivation to work on: jealousy. Some frail, in love with the Croft hambo, might have got hold of the blackmail reel for the purpose of busting up Leneta's romance with the guy—and, before doing this, decided to collect some shekels from the setup.

So I had to make sure Leneta was actually planning to marry Victor Croft. Then I'd know where to start.

WHEN I reached her sumptuous stash I hung around outside for damned near an hour before thumbing her doorbell. This was because I piped a sleek Cadillac convertible standing in the driveway. It was Croft's heap, and I didn't want to barge in on Leneta while he was on deck.

Presently I lamped him coming out. He didn't notice me lurking at the curb; and as soon as he wafted his swarthy good looks off the premises I made my play. Except for the maid who let me in, the Leonard chick was all alone in her wikiup. I ankled into the living room, fastened the fascinated glimpse on her.

She was a delishful little trick with more curves than the Burma Road. When she stood between me and the sunset streaming in through a window behind her, I got a swivel at the niftiest she-male silhouette I'd seen in a month of Mondays.

"I'm Dan Turner," I informed her. "Your friend Geoffrey Jackman was in to see me today."

She nodded listlessly. "He phoned, told me. He also mentioned the letter you received this morning."

"Nuts to the letter, hon. When was the last time you paid blackmail and how was it worked?"

"A w-week ago today. There was a note under my

door. It said to leave t-ten one thousand dollar b-bills in an envelope, slipped between the pages of Baedecker's Guide to Vienna on the shelves of the Hollywood Library at f-four in the afternoon. It promised the film would be delivered to me that night."

"You followed instructions?" I asked her.

"Y-yes. I got the bills from my bank; did exactly what the note demanded. But I didn't g-get the reel."

I nodded. Her story meshed with what I already knew. Which proved it was the blackmailer who had sent me the anonymous message and the three G-notes. That dough had been part of the Leonard doll's last payment.

The next problem was: how had the shakedown artist learned that Leneta was going to call on me for help?

I ELIMINATED Geoffrey Jackman. He'd come to hire me, not to steer me off. Leneta must have tipped her mitt to somebody else. I asked her point blank: "Aside from Jackman, did you mention to anybody that you were going to engage my services?"

"Why, no," she seemed puzzled. "That's wh-why I can't understand the letter you got. It w-worries me. Geoffrey's the only one who knew—" her voice trailed away.

Apparently there was nothing more I could learn

from her on that angle. So I switched my tactics, sat down alongside her on a big, deeply cushioned divan. I got confidential. "Look, sweet stuff. What would you do if I turned that reel over to you right now?"

I felt like a heel, raising her hopes that way. But I was after some pertinent information. She faced me, her peepers brimming with hope. "You—you mean you have it?"

"That depends," I said, and wormed my arm around her slender waist; hauled her close to me; her perfume drifted to my smeller, seeped into me—like a shot of cocaine.

I breathed in her ear: "Would you give up this Croft slob for a sleuth that makes pretty good dough? We could . . ."

She wriggled free; slammed me across the mush with her closed fist. It stung. "You—you dirty creep!" she gritted. "Take your hands off me!"

"Still in love with Croft, eh?" I sneered.

She darted across the room, picked up an andiron from the fireplace. "Get out. Get out before I brain you."

"Calm down, Beautiful," I grinned and set fire to a gasper. "I was just testing you, is all."

"Testing—?"

"Yeah. I wanted to know if you really love Croft."

She was still breathing hard. "You found out," she said grimly.

I admitted this, ruefully. I was almost sorry she hadn't fallen for my overtures. I liked her. But as long as she was another guy's private property there wasn't much I could do about it except wish I'd found her first.

I BLEW her a kiss; scrammed. The maid handed me my hat at the front door. I fixed the casual focus on this jane and she smiled back at me, not so casually. In fact, something told me she might be worth cultivating.

Right now was scarcely the time, though. So I tipped the quail a wink and hauled bunions.

Driving back to my office, I mulled things over. I knew now that Leneta Leonard and Victor Croft were leveling about their engagement; which gave me a hunch to play the jealousy possibility. One of Croft's discarded sweeties might be doing the blackmailing.

It was worth a toll call to New York. When I got to my quarters I dialed long distance; put through a connection to a columnist friend of mine in Manhattan who knew everything about everybody.

When I contacted him I said: "Hiya, chum. This is Turner talking from Hollywood, no less."

"Well, blow me down! What cooks, gumshoe?"

"I need some dope on a guy named Victor Croft. He's out here emoting in the yodeling snapshots; hasn't been on the coast long. I think he used to be on the stage, didn't he?"

"Sure. Played bits on Broadway. What about him?"

I said: "Who was his sweet patootie before he came west!"

"Let's see. Oh, yeah, I remember. Some dame named Dorothy Manton. A chorine. Yellow hair, lots of yumph. Followed him to Hollywood, I think. I understand he ditched her for Leneta Leonard. True?"

"Right," I said. "You could make a paragraph of it if you want to. But maybe I'll be slipping you something even hotter in a day or so." And I rang off.

Whereupon a voice behind me said: "Freeze, louse."

I twitched as if I'd been rammed with a hot corkscrew. There was something venomous, deadly, in that rasped command; a quality of menace that gave me goose pimples big enough to hang your hat on. Like a guy in a slow-motion movie, I turned on my heel; piped Geoffrey Jackman standing inside my office doorway.

WITH the black patch over one glim and a roscoe in his duke he resembled a pirate hankering to make me walk the plank. The rod was trained on my brisket, unwavering, ugly.

I said: "You've got me, bub. What's the gag!"

"If you don't know, you're not as smart as I

thought you were," he grated.

"Meaning what?"

"Meaning you're through. Washed up."

"With the Leneta Leonard case?"

"With any case."

I didn't like this. I thought fast; revised my entire conception of the whole mess. So it was Jackman, I thought, who was at the bottom of the deal. The pieces all fitted together like a completed jigsaw puzzle.

The Leonard cupcake had discussed hiring me with only one person: Jackman. Hence, he was the only guy in a position to send me the anonymous note I'd received that morning. The note had contained three one thousand dollar bills—which I'd traced back to Leneta as part of her last shakedown payoff. Then how else could Jackman have sent me those G-notes *unless he himself was the blackmailer?*

On the other hand, though, the one-eyed guy had come to me today, offered me a thousand fish to take the case. Why should he try to steer me off with an anonymous bribe, then attempt to hire me!

There was even an answer for this question when I put my grey matter to work. Jackman knew my rep; knew I'm in business for all the cash I can collect.. He had probably figured that I'd take the three grand to lay off, rather than accept a third of that sum to work on the case. His original visit had been to make sure; to hear me refuse to handle the mess.

But he'd overplayed his hand when he intimated that my effectiveness would be minimized. That had riled me, and I'd agreed to thrust my probe into the Leonard jane's troubles. Thus Jackman's psychological shenanigans had snapped back at him, kicked him in the teeth.

So now he was scared. And he had a cannon pointed at me.

The reason for his fright was obvious. He knew I was getting on the right track. He'd stood there just now, eavesdropped as I phoned New York about Victor Croft's former sweetie. If this particular bit of information bothered Jackman, it could only mean that he and the ex-sweetie were in cahoots. They were working together in the blackmail scheme.

All of which I added up in a split instant. I also realized I was in a ticklish spot as long as his heater was aimed at my cafeteria. So I did something about it.

I pulled an ancient gag on the guy; a gag they use in the detective magazines. It was corny, but it worked. I stared past my visitor, toward the door. "Hi, Bill!" I said. "You're just in the nick of time."

Of course there was nobody there. Jackman turned, though; and I grabbed the inkwell off my desk, fired it at him. It maced him on the back of the conk and he dropped like a cut rope.

I CATAPULTED over to him, unfastened his suspenders and used them to truss his wrists and gams. Then I propped him in a corner, put his rodney in my pocket, went back to the phone on my desk. I dialed Central Casting.

When they answered, I said: "You got a dame registered by the name of Dorothy Manton? Blonde. Lots of curves. Just out here a little while from Broadway. Chorus cutie."

In a moment I got my answer. I'd scored a bull's-eye with my guesswork. Central Casting has a list of everybody who ever worked in pix or hopes to work in pix. "Yep," the clerk told me. "I can give you her address and phone number."

"Do that," I said, and wrote the information on my scratch pad. Then I dialed the apartment joint where this Manton chicken lived.

The apartment switchboard op said Miss Manton was out but would be home around eleven that night, and did I care to leave a message?

"Never mind, hon," I said, and broke the connection. Then I turned, took a gander at Jackman. He was conscious. His glims were open and so were his ears. He'd overheard my inquiries.

I barged over to him. "You know what happens to eavesdroppers, pal?"

"No. What?"

"This," I growled, and tapped him on the thatch with my .32 automatic. He went limp in a hurry. I felt his cranium to make sure I hadn't fractured it. I hadn't. There were just a couple of lumps, one from my inkwell, one from my gat. He'd have a headache in the morning, but that was all.

I tightened the suspenders around his ankles and wrists, bestowed a curse on him and took a powder. Downstairs, I aimed my bucket back toward Leneta Leonard's igloo.

The blonde maid smiled at me when she opened up. "Miss Leonard has a visitor," she said.

I fished a five-spot out of my wallet, slipped it to the chick. "Stuff this in your sock and look the other way," I said. "Visitor or no visitor, I'm coming in." And I shoved past her; made my way to the living room.

The Leonard cutie got pale around the fringes when she piped me at the threshold. She was perched on the same davenport where I'd made that fake pass at her a few hours earlier. Aside from this, however, the scene had changed considerably. She now had a swarthy blister sitting beside her in a very chummy manner. He was Victor Croft.

Leneta flashed me the agonized swivel and I got hep to its meaning in short order. She was scared I'd open my trap, spill my adenoids about the blackmail setup. This would never do, with the Croft hambo present. He was the one guy in the world she didn't want in on the secret.

I PLAYED up to her. "Excuse me, Miss Leonard. I

didn't know you were busy. I just came to see you about the plans for redecorating your studio dressing room."

"Oh," she gave me a grateful smile. "I'll leave it entirely up to you, Mr. Smith," she improvised. Then she turned to Croft. "Victor, this is Mr. Smith, the interior decorator. Mr. Smith, of course you recognize Victor Croft. He's with Altamount."

I stuck out my mitt. The ham took it with the air of a king feeling the scales on a defunct fish. "How d'you do," he murmured in a bored tone.

I gushed all over him. "Mighty glad to meet you, Mr. Croft. I've seen you in pictures. You're swell." Then, to Leneta: "If everything's all right with you, Miss Leonard, I'll get right to work. I think I'll have the job finished by morning."

A pulse throbbed in her throat, "You m-mean it?"

I nodded, lammed. I was sure she'd understood my drift.

There was an opus I wanted to see at Grauman's Chinese, So I killed a couple of hours there, then moseyed to a groggery and inhaled a few snorts of Vat 69. Presently it was almost eleven o'clock—time for me to start rolling. I piled into my vee-eight, drove to the apartment stash where Dorothy Manton lived.

The automatic elevator whisked me up to her floor. I unholstered my gat, gumshoed to her portal, knocked.

The door opened. I shoved my roscoe forward and said: "Quite a trick, catching bullets with your kisser. You want to try it, maybe?"

The jane backed away. I barged in, kicked the door shut and got a good hinge at her puss. For once in my misspent career I was too flabbergasted to say anything.

And no wonder. The wren before me was Leneta Leonard's yellow-haired maid!

She found her voice first. "Wh-what's the idea?"

I said: "Pardon my curly tonsils, sister, but I crave that reel of film."

"Wh-what reel of film?" she quavered. Fear slithered into her optics, told me I was on the home stretch. "I don't know anything about a reel—"

"The devil you don't," I snapped. "It's the pic Leneta Leonard made a long time ago I'm talking about. You know, the one you've been using to blackmail her."

The blonde quail's glance shifted involuntarily and briefly to a bookcase standing against the far wall. I'd been keeping tab on her optics, waiting for just such a break.

She said: "You m-must be off your chump, Handsome."

"Yeah," I lifted a lip. "I lost my marbles trying to dope out this screwy tangle." And I moved toward the bookcase.

She tried to block me. "You can't—"

"Look, kiddo," I made my voice ugly. "See this thing in my duke? It's known professionally as a heater, or hog-leg if you read western stories. And if you think it's loaded with blanks, just start something. I dare you."

She backed up to a chair, sank into it. She was trembling like a cat coughing beef-seeds.

I OPENED the bookcase, dumped all the volumes out on the floor. Back in the corner of one shelf I found what I was after: a flat, round can of cinema celluloid. I opened it, held up a length of the reel so light would shine through. You could recognize the delishful doll who appeared in miniature on each transparent frame. It was Leneta Leonard.

"Nice," I said. "Very nice indeed."

The blonde maid blinked at me. "Look, Hawk-shaw. How would you like to make a deal?"

"I hear you talking," I said.

"We could cut you in on the gravy if you'd play ball with us on this thing," she made a coquettish mouth at me.

I said: "No dice, babe. In the first place, the Leonard jane is broke. You've bled her for all the traffic will bear. And in the second place I don't play with rats."

"You think I'm a rat?"

"Yeah. Dorothy Manton, she-male rodent. That's you. You were in love with Victor Croft back in New

York. You followed him here to Hollywood. He ditched you when he fell for Leneta. So you got sore; decided to do something about it. With Geoffrey Jackman's help, you located this reel of pix."

She said: "Smart, aren't you?"

"Smart enough. You and Jackman used the film for a shake-down. You probably figured to show the opus to Victor Croft when Leneta couldn't pay any more dough. That would wreck their wedding plans to hellangone. And just to keep an eye on your blackmail victim, you even wangled a job as her personal maid."

"All right," the blonde wren said sourly. "So now what happens to me?"

"You go to the cooler," I growled. "Jackman too. I've got him tied up in my office with his own suspenders. The two of you will serve a nice long stretch."

She stood up, swayed toward me. "Couldn't you give me a break, Handsome? If I paid back the blackmail money?"

I laughed at her, started to back toward the door. To my surprise she did nothing but step to the wall-switch and snap off the lights. I was still trying to figure her play when the front door of the stash swung open. You couldn't see it in the blackness, but you could hear the hinges creak.

Whereupon the blonde frail yeeped: *"I've got the dirty snoop! He almost glommed the film. Get him!"* And she clung to me, impeded my wild leap.

I swung the flat of my palm, bopped her on the chops. She let go, sagged back. I lunged toward the door just as a roscoe sneezed: *Ka-chow!* and spat a streak of orange flame in my general direction.

The slug missed me. I made a dig for my own shoulder-holstered gat—and found the holster empty. The yellow-haired Manton minx had glommed it when she had hung the grab on me.

Even as I discovered this, she started triggering. I ducked for a corner as the cannon belched its thunderous bellow. And then I heard a groan, a gurgle and the thump of somebody slumping to the floor.

The blonde chick quit firing. "Which—which one did I hit? Somebody say something!"

Instead of answering, I slithered across the room on all fours; ran into a prone figure I couldn't see. But I could find the guy's wrist; and I could feel that his pulse wasn't beating. He was deader than fried fishcakes.

Which was my cue to lam—fast This defunct monkey had been creamed with my heater; and that would look plenty bad for me if the cops found it out. I straightened up, dived across the room by instinct, collided with the Manton dame.

She had my gat in one mitt, the can of film in the other. I punched her in the kisser, knocked her colder than January at the North Pole. I got the roscoe and the movie reel, pivoted, catapulted to the window. I raised the sash, went over the sill and down the fire escape to my jalopy.

It was midnight when I pulled up in front of Leneta Leonard's lavish igloo in Beverly. There was a light burning downstairs as I made for the porch, fingered the bell. She probably had Victor Croft in there with her, I figured.

Not that it mattered. All I intended to do was hand her the can of film, then beat it without saying anything.

I rang again. Presently the door opened—and for the second time that night I got a shock. The guy standing before me was Geoffrey Jackman.

HE had a bandage around his noggin, and his one good peeper blazed like a four-alarm fire fueled with hate. He said: "You lousy son!" and lunged at me.

I sidestepped, glued the grab on him, pinioned him and gasped: "What gives?"

"Let go!" he choked. "Turn me loose so I can kill you!"

"Stew that kind of talk, bub. How did you get here? I thought you were—"

"Yeah. You thought you had me tied up in your office, you filthy heel. You thought you could come out here and make some more passes at Leneta!" he caterwauled.

I began to see daylight. "So that's it!" I said. Then

I yelled into the house. "Hey, Miss Leonard. Come take this crazy jerk off me! I've got a present for you."

The cuddly cinema cupcake came to the door, her puss as white as fresh laundry. "Something . . . for m-me . . .?"

I freed one hand, reached inside my coat, tossed the can of movie spool at her. "There's what you wanted, hon."

Droplets of brine started running out of her lamps, streaking her map with mascara. "You . . . you g-got . . .!"

"Yeah," I said, and shoved Geoffrey Jackman away from me. He had a stupid look on his mush. "Funny," I growled at him. "I had an idea *you* were behind this deal. You pulled a gun on me in my office—"

He blushed sheepishly. "That was because you'd tried to get fresh with Leneta. I was jealous."

"Then why did you try to mow me down in Dorothy Manton's wikiup?" I yelped.

"Me? I've been here since ten-thirty. When I got away from your office 1 came right to Leneta. Ask Victor Croft. He was just leaving as I arrived. He'll prove it."

But the swarthy Croft hambo would never prove anything. Inside the Leonard doll's stash a radio was already blotting: "Extra flash! Victor Croft, the new film star, was just found shot to death in the apartment of an extra girl named Dorothy Manton, who has disappeared—"

That's right. It was Croft who got cooled in the darkness of the blonde wren's joint. Croft was the blackmailer. He'd never intended to marry Leneta. He merely made her fall for him so he could use that movie reel to shake her down for a stack of shekels.

His real sweetie was the Manton jane. He'd even planted her as Leneta's maid to keep in touch with things. She was the one that overheard Leneta and Jackman discussing the proposition of hiring me; which explained the anonymous note I'd received.

And now Croft was deceased; his own hot mama had browned him. Which was poetic justice.

The funny thing is, the cops never did nab that blonde bimbo. She simply dropped out of sight. And I'm not saying anything to anybody. Neither is Geoffrey Jackman. He's married now to Leneta Leonard, and they're perfectly willing to let sleeping dogs lie!

# ARROW FROM NOWHERE

There was only one man on the set who could have shot the arrow, yet Dan hated to think Jeff could be guilty. Motive tumbles over motive, and suspect waltzes around with suspect—but there still remains the question: Where did the arrow come from?

H E CAME swinging through the property trees like a muscular brown streak, straight toward the cameras that were grinding at the edge of the giant sound stage. I had to give the guy credit; he was plenty good at his specialty. He reminded me of a sleek ape-man as he bounded from branch to branch.

Which was exactly what he was supposed to be. For more than four years Vance Vannister had been playing the leading role in Pinnacle Pic's famous "King of the Jungle" series of which this present opus was the latest thrilling installment. His face was ruggedly handsome, he wore his hair long, and in his tiger skin costume he looked like the answer to an old maid's dream. As I watched his gyrations from the sidelines I found myself envying his athletic build, his slick gymnastic skill, the tawny suntan that made him resemble some mythical bronze god without benefit of grease paint. Even the bow and quiver of arrows slung over his ungarnished shoulder seemed part of him.

There were other things I envied about Vannister, too. There wasn't another actor in Hollywood with as many girl friends. He merely had to smile at a doll and it was practically all over.

"What a guy!" I whispered to Sally Sprague standing alongside me.

Sally made a bitter mouth. She was directing this jungle melodrama; one of the few she-males ever to achieve megaphone status in the galloping tintypes. She'd come up the hard way: secretary to a scenario writer, then script clerk, then doctor of limping dialogue, third assistant director, and finally a chance at short subjects. From there she made the big jump to feature lengths and a shot at "King of the Jungle."

She said: "You mean what a heel," without taking

her ice-grey glims off the action in front of her.

I pinned the puzzled focus on her. She was a competent-looking cupcake in her late twenties or early thirties, at a guess; brown hair done in a bun at

the nape of her neck, a nice profile, clear complexion, a figure that was just right—although her man-tailored whipcord outfit didn't do it full justice.

THE Sprague chick and her stunt expert hubby had been my personal friends for a long time; which was why I was visiting this huge Pinnacle set now. When the present scene was finished, I had a date to take Sally and Jeff out to supper. I hadn't known she disliked her handsome star, though. It startled me just a little.

"In what way is Vannister a heel?" I asked her.

"He gets too free and easy with women where it's not appreciated."

"Meaning you, hon?"

"Me," she said. "Among others."

"With him it's a habit," I grinned."

"Somebody may cure him of it one of these days. Permanently." Then she added: "Let's stop this whispering. The mikes might pick it up on the sound track."

By that time the Vannister hambo had dropped down to earth and was moving carefully through the prop underbrush, mugging into the lenses. As an actor he stank to heaven, but you don't have to act when you're a gorgeous chunk of man.

As he skulked closer, Sally nodded a signal. Her husband was perched on a high parallel over the stage, above the camera lines. Jeff Sprague was stocky, bald, the most unromantic looking specimen this side of a hobo's convention. He knew his stuff, though. There wasn't a stunt in the celluloid book he couldn't do.

Right now he had a bow and arrow in his mitts. He aimed, let fly. The arrow flashed past Vance Vannister's noggin; missed him by a whisker and twanged into a tree exactly where Sprague had intended it to go.

The handsome ham registered anger; gave vent to a God-awful screech. It was his trade mark, that guttural yeep; just about the only dialogue they ever wrote in the script for him. He slithered sidewise; whereupon the ground seemed to open up and gulp him like a raw oyster.

That was part of the rehearsed action, too. According to the scenario, jungle natives had dug a lion trap—a deep pit camouflaged by sticks and twigs and leaves. Vannister was to fall in this hole, thereby meeting the heroine of the opus.

I'D WATCHED the first rehearsal a while ago. The heroine in question was a cookie named Elayne Lorton, a brunette newcomer to the yodeling snapshots. Some Pinnacle talent scout had discovered her in a middle western circus, signed her up, shipped her to the coast as possible starring material. The studio had cast her opposite Vannister to try her out.

Now she stood in the bottom of the pit as lion

bait, trussed to an upright stake with her arms firmly bound behind her, clad in a leopard skin. The idea was for Vannister to drop down beside her, lamp her predicament, untie her, and rescue her from the trap. That part of the action would take place after the cameras had been moved to the brink of the hole for a downward angle shot.

So he took his cue; vanished from view. Sally Sprague started to call: "Cut."

She never got the word out of her kisser, though, because all of a sudden a terrified she-male scream knifed upward out of the depths, raw, harsh, shrill enough to peel the fur off a brass monkey. The instant I heard it I smelled trouble. The yeep hadn't been play-acting. It was the McCoy.

I said: "What the—!" and plunged onto the set, reached the pit, squinted down. What I saw sent an ugly sensation slugging clear through me.

The brunette Elayne Lorton was squirming against the wide leather thongs that bound her to the stake. And all the while she was howling: "My God—look—oh-h-h, my God!"

Vance Vannister was stretched out in front of her, handsome as ever in his sun-tan and breech clout. But he was all through with the ladies. The arrows had spilled out of the quiver he carried, and one feather-tipped shaft was sticking out of his manly bellows—the barbed end buried six inches deep. By the time I dropped down to feel his pulse, there

wasn't any.

The jungle king was deader than prohibition.

I STRAIGHTENED up, barged to the black-haired cupcake, plucked at her fetters. She sagged against them, which made them all the tighter. "Loosen up, babe!" I rasped.

"I—I th-think I'm g-going to f-faint!"

"Save it for later." I snapped her out of it by feeding her a sharp stinger across the chops. Then, as she stiffened, I snarled: "What happened?"

"I d-don't know! Vance dropped down. Then,

suddenly, he was lying there w-with that arrow th-through him!"

"You mean one fell out of his quiver and he skewered himself on it by accident?"

"I tell you I don't know! Maybe it was that. Or m-maybe the arrow was sh-shot at him—"

I blinked at the Lorton cutie. "Shot at him?"

"How can I tell? It all happened s-so quickly—please g-get me out of here!" Then two different things took place at the same time. First I got the leather thongs unfastened. And second, she swooned in my arms.

Under any other circumstances I'd have enjoyed holding her. But I didn't have time for that now, because there was a defunct actor at my feet and elev-enteen dozen assorted faces squinting down into the hole, watching me.

I lifted the inert brunette jessie; passed her up over the lip of the pit. There were plenty of hands willing to grab onto her: bit players, cameramen, sound technicians, juicers. It wasn't every evening in the week they got a chance to get that close to Elayne Lorton. And she was too unconscious to pick her rescuers now.

I piped a bald dome in the throng, with a map under it that was seven shades of pale. "Okay, Jeff. Jump down here a minute," I said.

Sally Sprague's stunt expert hubby landed on the balls of his brogans alongside me. "Wh-what is it?

How did it—?"

"That's what I crave to know," I said in an undertone. "Did you twang a barb through the guy's ticker?"

"Me? Good Lord, Sherlock, what makes you ask that?"

"Sally told me Vannister had been making passes at her. She happens to be your wife. You're tops with a bow and arrow. Figure it out for yourself."

A peculiar expression slithered into Jeff Sprague's narrowed optics. "I get it. You're accusing me."

"Not accusing, pal. Asking."

"It's the same thing. But you won't make it stick, understand? You won't frame me for this kill." Then, before I could guess his intention, he brought a haymaker up from around his ankles; planted it on my button.

He tagged me and I didn't even see it coming; didn't get the chance to duck. My knees turned to boiled noodles and I dropped like a cut rope. I was blacked out.

SOMEBODY dribbled a jolt of cheap bourbon down my Sunday gullet and I woke up strangling. During my slumbers I'd been hoisted out of the hole to stage level with my noggin reposing on a clump of property bushes. I opened my glims, stared into the beefy mush of my friend, Dave Donaldson from the homicide squad.

Dave's headquarters minions were all over the set like an infestation of ants around a heap of sugar. I piped a pair of morgue orderlies loading Vance Vannister's husk into a wicker meat basket, carting him away; saw the Lorton doll on the receiving end of first aid from a police surgeon. Sally Sprague stood nearby, looking grim; but her hubby wasn't anywhere in sight. Evidently he'd lammed after bopping me, whereupon somebody had beefed to the bulls.

Donaldson stopped dosing me with whiskey and said: "That's better, Hawkshaw. I thought you were going to stay asleep all night. What did Sprague tag you with, brass knucks?"

"Just his bare duke," I sat up groggily, rubbed my unhinged jaw. "It was plenty potent." Then I mumbled: "You've got the dragnet out for him?"

Dave nodded. "He won't get far. You think he's the one that fired the arrow, do you?"

"How do I know? Maybe he was just scared the circumstantial evidence would railroad him."

"You needn't be loyal just because he happened to be a friend of yours," Dave grunted. "Friendship and killery don't mix."

I said: "As a rule they don't. But maybe Vannister accidentally butched himself. Maybe an arrow bounced out of his quiver and he fell on it."

"Nuts! His weight would have busted the shaft in that case, or anyhow ruined the feathers."

"All right. If the thing was shot from a bow, Jeff's your guy. I hate to say it, though." I swayed to my pins, fished out a gasper from my crumpled pack, set fire to it. "Could anyone else on the stage have done the dirty work?"

"Nobody near the cameras—which eliminates Sally Sprague and her technical crew. Miss Lorton is out, of course; she was tied to a stake in the pit. Nobody on the set proper, either; the arrow had too much of a downward slant. It came from up high."

"Sprague was on a high platform parallel," I admitted.

Dave scratched his chin-stubble. "That's what worries me, gumshoe. We found another target bow on an electricians' catwalk up near the rafters. Three or four juicers were up there handling the arcs and spotlights. I'm trying to be fair about this." He scowled. "We're holding those guys for questioning."

"I hope you get somewhere. Me, I'm not interested. How's for letting me haul bunions? There's nothing I can do around here, as far as I can see."

HE GAVE me the office and I scrammed. But just as I was circling the set and making for an exit, a voice called: "Dan. Wait a minute."

I turned. Sally Sprague was in an alcove formed by two piles of painted scenery, beckoning to me. She had a queer expression on her map, harried, worried.

She didn't look like a competent, self-assured she-male director now. Somehow she seemed more feminine in spite of her man-tailored outfit.

I SAID: "Yeah, kiddo?" and moved toward her.

She gave me the frantic focus. "From where I stood, I could hear what you said to Lieutenant Donaldson. I appreciate the w-way you tried to protect Jeff." Her smile was a twisted grimace. "It was decent of you, after he'd slugged you so hard."

"I've been slugged before, Sally. I'm used to it."

"You're not sore?"

"Not particularly. If Jeff's guilty, I'm sorry. If he's innocent, he'll go free and I won't hold a grudge."

She took a step closer to me. "That's not like you, Dan, to be neutral. Usually you take sides. But violently."

"Are you asking me to take sides now?"

"I wish you would."

"For or against your hubby?"

"That's a foolish question. I love Jeff. I want him cleared. I can't stand to think of . . . Oh-h-h, Dan . . . isn't th-there anything to be d-done for him?" Abruptly she nestled in my arms. Two enormous tears spilled out of her peepers, skidded down her complexion.

I wasn't taking advantage when I kissed her. I was just being friendly.

She seemed to take it that way. "You know what

I'm asking you to d-do, don't you, Dan?"

"I can guess. You want me to go to bat for Jeff, get him out from under the rap."

"Yes. I—I'll pay you your fee. Whatever you say."

I said: "Look, hon. I wouldn't take pay from you. Money, marbles, chalk or anything."

"Meaning just what?" the crooked grin twisted her puss again.

"Meaning you're, first of all, a pal." I proved this by kissing her again. . . . Then I drew back. "And don't ever think you haven't got what it takes to drive a man off his chump. Vance Vannister was crazy about you, wasn't he?" And he had first call on the whole Hollywood crop. Don't underrate your-self"

"Vannister!" her whisper was sharp, bitter. "If I hadn't told you about his attentions, you wouldn't have thought to accuse Jeff."

"I didn't accuse Jeff, hon. I asked him a question and he lost his head, was all. I wish to Whozit I could finger somebody else for the Vannister bump. I'd jump at the chance to do it for free. But—"

"Suppose I give you an angle to work on?"

"If you've got one, let's have it."

"Mike Clancy, my head electrician. He was top-side on that catwalk where they found a spare bow."

"Clancy!" I said. "He's seven years older than Noah. His wife must be in her fifties. Don't tell me Vannister was giving her the rush."

"No. They have a daughter though. Kitty Clancy. She plays bits on this lot. Vannister made eyes at her, I know. You've heard of fathers protecting a daughter, haven't you?"

I said: "I'll be a so-and-so!" and swung around on my heel. "Be seeing you, Sally." And I lammed out of the building, made for my parked jalopy, went tearing hellity-blip off the Pinnacle lot.

KITTY CLANCY was a flip, blatant-looking redhead who'd pulled out of the home nest, set herself up in

an apartment on Franklin. Or maybe somebody else had helped; her salary wouldn't easily have handled the set-up.

She had sultry glims, a pouting kisser with a cigarette dangling from the lower lip, when she answered to my knock. Helpfully enough, we knew each other casually; we'd met on a few parties but I'd never dated her. I try to steer clear of the gold-digger type.

She said: "Well, handsome, what cyclone dropped you on my doorstep?"

"Hi, Toots." I shouldered past her into the living room. "You alone?"

She grinned wisely. "Not now I'm not."

I let that pass. I said: "Skip it, sweet stuff. I didn't mean to insinuate anything. I could use a drink," I added.

"Why didn't you bring a bottle, then? My friends always do."

I saw I wasn't getting anywhere by pretending to be interested in making whoopee. "So okay," I said. "So I didn't bring a bottle and I'm just snooping around."

"That's what I thought. Who you checking up on?"

"You, principally. And Vance Vannister."

"Oh. That louse. Don't tell me he's in Dutch or I'll bust out laughing." The way she said this made it apparent that she hadn't heard about the ham's death. That was to be expected, however. The murder had happened less than an hour ago, actually; and Kitty didn't look like the kind of dame that nags her radio dials for a news broadcast every fifteen minutes. If she read the papers as much as once a month, it would be strictly for the various gossip columns.

I said: "You wouldn't mind seeing Vannister caught in a jam, hunh?"

"I'd love it—after the way he treated me."

"How was that?"

"How does he treat any woman? He's a quick storm catching you without your umbrella. You get drenched, and you love it. Then all of a sudden it's over and you're standing in a cold wind, shivering in the dark." She ankled to her kitchenette, came back with a fifth of Scotch and two glasses. "I'm buying you a drink, Hawkshaw. Consider yourself honored, because it's against all my principles." She poured two drinks.

THE Scotch wasn't my favorite brand, but it was almost as good. "You stock nice stuff, babe," I said.

"It don't cost me anything."

"The same for this apartment stash?"

"Good guess."

"Vannister pays the rent?" I probed.

She laughed harshly. "He's got the first dime he ever borrowed off some dumb Dora. No, chum.

Vannister has nothing to do with this joint. I moved here after he waved me good-bye."

"You lived at home before that, eh?"

"Sure. I'd hardly had a real date before Vannister. Afterward, when my old man and old lady tumbled to the score, they kicked me out on my elbows. I landed right side up," she added.

"Your parents don't care what happens to you?"

"Not unless I drop dead. That'd please them. They'd say it was heaven's judgment on my sins— meaning vindication of their bigoted opinion. Say, why do I beat my chops to you this way? You must have slipped me a shot of truth serum."

I said: "Not at all. You're telling me things I need to know. For instance, that your father wouldn't care enough about you to take it out on Vannister."

"My old man? He's too spineless to walk on his feet. He crawls around on his belly like a worm." She tensed. "What do you mean, take it out on Vannister? In what way?"

"The guy's defunct, hon," I gave it to her straight. "Someone shot an arrow through him on the set this evening. We thought it might have been your dad."

"Vannister croaked? Vance Vannister?"

"Yeah."

I've been a Hollywood snoop for a hell of a lot of years and I thought I'd seen everything; but the Clancy quail reached down in the grab-bag, pulled out something brand new to me. She started to laugh, weirdly, silently. It was genuine merriment, sardonic and extremely unpleasant to watch. "He's dead and you want to pin it on my sniveling pop! Sherlock, I love you for that. I love you because you've brought me the happiest news I ever had. You and I are going to celebrate. Now." She raised her glass, drained it. "Nails in Vannister's casket. Cyanide for my old man. And . . . kisses for you, handsome. But kisses."

She dragged me down alongside her on the davenport, lifted her crimson yap to mine.

I yelped: "Hey, what the—!" and tried to pry myself out of the tangle.

AS SOON as I could fight free, I helped myself to another snort of Scotch. "You seem pleased in strange ways, babe," I said.

The red-haired wren grinned. She reminded me of a cat purring over spilled cream. "I'll like it even better when you put my old gent in the bastile."

"That probably won't happen. You practically cleared him by the things you told me. If he kicked you out of your home, he certainly wouldn't give a hoot about your boy friend. Not enough to cool the guy, anyhow."

She frowned. "No, I suppose not, come to think about it. But I wish you'd quit calling Vannister my boy friend. That ended a long while ago, when he took up with his new leading lady."

"That brunette chick? Elayne Lorton?"

"Yep. She's the one that beat my time."

I said: "And from her, the hambo jumped to Sally Sprague—or tried to. Which brings me right back to Jeff Sprague?"

"Why?"

"I'm trying to clear him. He's a friend of mine."

"Well, then, look. Why don't you go see the Lorton jane? Maybe she knows more than she's telling." Kitty smiled knowingly. "Even if she don't know anything, it might pay you to call on her. Maybe she'd like to celebrate Vannister's death, too."

I got my hat, blew Kitty a kiss, scrammed. When I got downstairs and opened the door of my jalopy, Jeff Sprague himself was sitting in it. He had a rod in his mitt, aimed at my favorite adenoids.

"GET in, Turner," he said. "I want to talk to you."

I goggled at him. "How the blazes did you get here?"

"Saw your car as I passed. Come on, snoop. Drive."

I obeyed; couldn't do anything else as long as he had the drop on me. "This is no way to be chummy," I said.

"Nuts to the sentiment. I want to know what was behind something you spilled in that sound stage pit. About Vannister and my wife. I want to know your reasons for accusing me."

"I didn't accuse you, Jeff. I just asked you. And there wasn't anything between Sally and that handsome louse. He made passes; but she brushed them off."

"Who told you?"

"Sally herself. She was leveling. She even hired me to get you clear if I could. She knows you had no cause for jealousy."

"Vannister was pestering her, was he? I never suspected that."

"Then you had no reason to bump him," I said.

He was silent for several blocks. Then: "Sally might have had a reason, though. She's a funny girl. I've seen her blaze up at a lot of guys for getting fresh with her. And hold the grudge, afterward."

"That's a normal reaction, isn't it?" I said.

"Not with Sally," he seemed almost to be talking to himself instead of to me. "She's never told me, but I think she must have had a peculiar experience of some sort when she was a kid. Something ugly that warped her a little, inside."

I took a sidewise swivel at him. "Meaning she's slightly minus her marbles? Don't be a dope."

"Call it a psychological quirk. Tell me, Dan. Do you consider Sally . . . attractive?"

I didn't like the question, considering that it came from a husband with a gat in his fist. "Sure," I said warily. "Sure she's attractive. In her way."

He said: "And yet you've noticed she always

wears man tailored clothes?"

"I've noticed."

"She wears them for a reason. She doesn't want men to fall for her. At home she . . . she's very different." He groped for the words. "I'm trying to tell you she never lets her guard down, outside. Tailored suits. No makeup. A director's job—not a feminine occupation. Sally's afraid of men."

I kept driving. "So she's afraid of men. So what?"

"So she could hate any guy who really hurt her. Hate him enough to . . ."

"You're building up a nice case against her, Jeff."

He thought this over. "No, I'm not," he said presently. "I'm just letting you know Sally's innocent. You see, *I* murdered Vance Vannister. I plugged him with an arrow because he was bothering my wife. You can take me to headquarters now."

I drew over to the curb in front of an apartment on North Vine. "Very funny," I grunted at him. "Very funny indeed. Your noggin might just as well be made of glass, bub. Anybody can see the cogs going around. You've come to the conclusion Sally butched Vannister for a psychopathic motive, and you love her so much that you don't want her to take the rap. So you're willing to take it for her."

"No, really, I—"

"It stinks, Jeff. I don't believe you."

"The cops will. They're the ones that count."

I said: "You really want to frame yourself, do

you?"

"I want to take my medicine for something I did."

"For something you think Sally did," I corrected him. "Suppose I prove to you she couldn't possibly have chilled the guy? Would you retract your phony confession in that case?"

"You'll have to show me."

"I think I can do that. I was standing directly beside her when Vannister dropped down into the pit. She gave him his cues; but she wasn't toting anything that remotely resembled a bow and arrow. I tell you her hands were empty."

"You could be lying."

I shrugged. "Okay, stupid. See this apartment wigwam? Elayne Lorton lives here. I was on my way to interview her when I found you in my chariot. Now you can come along."

"What for?" he asked me suspiciously.

"The Lorton cupcake was tied to a stake in the pit. Vannister was croaked before her very glims. I want you to hear what she's got to say."

"I'll go on one condition."

"Yeah? Name it?"

"Phone the cops. Right now. Tell them to come pick me up. I'm tired dodging every policeman I see. Then I'll listen to the Lorton girl while they're on their way here. If anything Miss Lorton says will clear Sally, then I'll fight for my freedom in court— take my chances. But if Sally's in the middle, I'll confess until they convict me."

Love does funny things to some guys. With Jeff Sprague, it seemed to give him a martyr complex. For once in my life I was tackling a homicide beef in an effort to save a client who actually craved to take the jolt. The thing was so screwy it gave me a headache.

I said: "Slip me your roscoe and let's go. We'll phone the law from the lobby."

He looked pleased at this. He even gave me a nickel to drop in the slot when I dialed Dave Donaldson.

THE Lorton cupcake was alone in her igloo when I rapped; not only alone but evidently trying to woo forty winks. Her lounging pajamas were of the heavy Chinese silk variety, white and glossy. A midnight waterfall of wavy black tresses fell around her shoulders to make attractive contrast against the pajama jacket and against a puss just about as white.

"Y-yes?" she hung the tearstained gaze on me. Then she spotted Sprague. "You—!" she caterwauled. And all of a sudden she flurried at him with her claws digging at his profile.

Her abrupt attack on the guy caught me flat-footed; took Sprague by surprise, too. Before he could duck, she raked a set of furrows down his chops. Ketchup dribbled into his collar as he gasped: "Hey, what—?"

"You k-killed the man I loved!" she yodeled. "You shot an arrow through him! I'll make you suffer for it, too!" She scratched him again, this time on his balding sconce.

I recovered from my flabbergasted attitude; lunged at her and dragged her backward into the room. She kicked at me furiously but it didn't buy her anything.

Sprague blinked at her as he mopped his leaking features with a handkerchief. "You—you think I did it, eh?"

"I know you did! Who else could have?"

His voice lowered tensely. "Explain that."

"The arrow came from up over the set. I remembered, after I got over my shock. I saw it."

I said: "See, Jeff? Now maybe you'll believe me when I tell you Sally's in the clear."

"My God," the words were thick in his gullet. "My God. The cops are coming. I forced you to call them. I wanted to shield my w-wife. But she doesn't need shielding. She's innocent. And so am I—b-but I'll be railroaded—" He whirled. "I'm getting out!"

For an instant I was on the verge of letting him lam. Then I realized it would make a fool of me. I'd phoned the law, told them I had Jeff under glass. If he escaped, it would poke holes in my reputation big enough to garage a freight train.

Moreover, if he pulled another duck-out it would be another circumstantial evidence of his guilt, false but damning. He'd be much better off in the clink, fighting the case legally while I snooped around for the genuine killer. No matter how you looked at it, and no matter how much I disliked the job, it was up to me to hold him; turn him in.

I made a regretful fist, jumped him, lowered the boom on him. My knuckles massaged him on the whiskers, dropped him like a chopped log. I dug out my handcuffs, nippered his left wrist, started to put the other bracelet on his right while he was taking a count of ten.

Then the Lorton quail shrilled vindictively, circled me, tried to fasten herself on his recumbent poundage. "Now I've got him! Now I'll get even with him for—"

I sighed: "Oh, for gosh sake!" and hauled her off "Why not behave, babe? Sprague didn't cool Vannister. And even if he did, I can't see what difference it'd make to you. The ham had already fed you the brush-off."

"I loved him. He'd have c-come back to me. Let me g-go!"

I toted her into the inner room, tossed her into a big chair. Then, because I'd already used my cuffs on Jeff Sprague, I had to yank a tasseled drapery cord from the window to tie her up.

Even as I finished the job I heard Sprague scrambling to his gams in the front room; lurching toward the door. I dived after him, nabbed him by the free dangling handcuff—the one I hadn't had a chance to fasten to his right wrist. I copped a gander around but didn't pipe anything heavy enough to link him to. The furniture was period stuff, pretty flimsy: a Louis the Umpteenth table, some chairs, a chaise longue built for midgets, an escritoire that deserved the name because it wasn't hefty enough to be called a desk. It had a scrapbook and a lamp on it, the lamp's pastel shade matching the carpet on the floor; but nothing around which to click Sprague's spare handcuff.

So I pushed him into the inner room, attached him to a radiator, right near the spot where Elayne Lorton was trussed like a gorgeous mummy. Then I left, to wait for Dave Donaldson's arrival at the front door of the flat.

"You two be good children or I'll slap the non-sense out of both of you," I said as I barged off. Neither of them answered me. I hardly expected them to.

IN THE living room I fired a gasper, tried to draw inspiration from the fumes. I was convinced Jeff hadn't chilled Vance Vannister. Neither had his frau. The elderly electrician, Clancy, was equally in the clear on the basis of the story his red-haired daughter Kitty had told me. The Lorton jane had been tied up just as securely in the bottom of the sound stage pit as she was now, which put her out of the running in the suspicion sweepstakes. So who the devil had skewered the vain, handsome Vannister ham?

It would be terrific if his croakery turned out to have been an accident after all, I thought. I started thumbing idly through the scrapbook on the escritoire, looking at the faded press clippings without really seeing them. Suppose an arrow had fallen out of Vannister's quiver when he dropped into the pit? Suppose he had actually impaled himself on the barb—

My glim fell on a newspaper publicity item dealing with a middle western circus. And as I tabbed it, the front door smacked open; Dave Donaldson lumbered into the room. At the same precise instant there came a she-male screech from inside.

It was Elayne Lorton's shrill bleep. "Quick—he's committing suicide—"

Then a hoarse cry from Jeff Sprague, ugly, doom-ridden. I was already catapulting toward the door and yowling for Donaldson to follow me. "Come on, dopey! It's the payoff!"

Dave tugged at his service .38 and wheezed: "Hunh?"

Then I flew through the doorway with my superchargers whining. "Freeze, you she-devil! Get her, Dave. Get the Lorton cupcake before she pulls another kill!"

Donaldson triggered from the hip. His roscoe bellowed: *Ka-chow!* and the trussed brunette sagged backward with a slug through her leg. A knife clattered to the floor and rasping moans came out of Jeff Sprague's constricted gullet where the sharp shiv had already nicked a shallow slice, not quite deep enough to reach his jugular. He couldn't get away because he was nippered to the radiator.

"My God! She—she tried to cut my throat with—with her—" his voice trailed off stupidly.

Donaldson looked idiotic. "I fired without thinking. This'll cost me my badge. How could the wren have stabbed this bozo when you've got her arms tied behind her?"

I said: "With her bare feet, pal."

"Wh-wha-what?"

Sprague gulped. "It's true! She—she—"

I said: "I just got the tip-off from a publicity clipping in the dame's scrapbook. She used to be with a small circus before a Pinnacle talent scout picked her up as movie material."

"Curse you!" the Lorton doll howled. "You can't—"

"Oh, but I can, babe," I told her grimly. "Your circus specialty was a peculiar one. You were a contortionist with a side show. *You could do almost as many things with your bare feet and toes as the average person does with his hands.*"

She called me all the names in the alphabet.

I LET her keep yapping until her mainspring ran down and the slug in her leg began to hurt. Then I

124

said: "You beefed Vannister because he gave you a play and then handed you the ozone. When he dropped into the pit on that sound stage this evening, you had an airtight alibi; you were trussed to an upright stake with your arms tied behind you. But actually your bare tootsies were loose; and they were all you needed. You picked an arrow out of the guy's quiver, rammed it through him—with your educated toes."

"Get me a doctor—I'm bleeding to death—"

"Then, a minute ago, when I had you tied up again, you pulled a shiv from somewhere with your feet; tried to slice Jeff Sprague's throat to look like suicide. It would have closed the Vannister case with Jeff guilty by his own apparent confession—and he'd have been much too deceased to deny it."

"I—admit everything—call a doctor—"

That was all I needed. I turned to Donaldson. "You take it from here, Dave," I said. Then I unlocked Sprague and we ankled down to my bucket, drove home to his stash.

So I took them out to supper, after all. And later I left them; blipped myself to Kitty Clancy's wikiup. That red-haired wren and I had some more celebrating to take care of. . . .

# FEATURE SNATCH

The idea was new—and was tops! Whoever thought of stealing a million dollar production before it was released? And behind it was the ransom angle, and there was blackmail, too. Sometimes a detective likes to get his teeth into a case like that. It's like matching your wits with a genius.

NOBODY got killed, but it was a major miracle. The two jalopies smacked together with a thunder of a crash; rebounded with their front ends dripping bolts and rivets. Headlight glass showered the road like a rain of razors.

The night was late and there was a lot of fog. I'd been over to a Pasadena movie house catching a sneak preview of the latest Supertone costume opus, a stinker costing copious kopecks, and I was headed back toward Hollywood after the show when this smashup happened. I lamped the whole thing because it took place spang in front of me.

I was driving across Pasadena's famous Suicide Bridge, with a big black Cad sedan just ahead of my bucket. As the Cad reached the far end of the bridge, a roadster without headlights darted out of a foggy side-road, hellity-blip; lurched smack into the sedan's path.

The Cad swerved, tried to miss a collision, failed. I jammed on my own anchors; skidded to a squealing stop just as metal met metal with a crunching

**127**

noise you could have heard all the way to Glendale. The sedan ploughed broadside into the offending roadster. Then both machines were suddenly motionless.

I said: "What the—!" and bounced to the pavement to see if there was anything I could do. At first

I figured an ambulance would be needed—maybe even a hearse.

My own headlamps spotlighted the two wrecked machines and I glommed a gander at the roadster's driver. She was a young and very shapely quail with yellow hair and nifty gams. At that very instant she slid from her ruined buggy and started running into the fog.

Then the darkness gulped her like a raw oyster.

At the same instant, the Cad sedan's driver popped out of his car the way a slice of bread erupts from an automatic toaster. He was short, slight, about the size of a jockey, and he was giving vent to fervent cuss-words. He yelled: "— — —! Come back here!"

He began pelting after the blonde chick and I raced along beside him. I've got no sympathy for carelessness at a steering wheel regardless of age, sex or beauty—and the accident had been entirely the yellow-haired wren's fault. I intended to nab her if I could. She deserved to have her shapely form deposited in the nearest jug.

AS I overtook and passed the little bozo, I whipped out my pencil flashlight; sprayed its beam through the fog. There was no trace of the blonde babe, though. She'd probably taken cover somewhere; might be hiding down in the bushes of the Arroyo Seco by this time. There wasn't much chance of finding her in the thickening fog without a regiment of searchers.

I halted, and the jockey-sized punk panted up to me. He had a skinny puss, a sharp needle of a nose, and his glims gave out sparks. "See her anywhere?"

"Nope."

"Well, come on! Let's smoke her out!"

"Not much use trying it, pal," I said regretfully. "She took a perfect powder, I'm afraid."

"Dammit, what am I going to do, let her get away with this?"

I said: "Not necessarily. You can get her name from the roadster's registration certificate and sue to the limit. I'll be glad to appear in court for you if you like. My name's Dan Turner. I'm a private eye in Hollywood."

I handed him my card. He took it; traded me a grateful glance. "Thanks a lot. I've heard of you, Mr. Turner. You see, I'm Spence Hanley."

"Nephew and sole heir of Ben Hanley, the high mogul of Supertone Pix?"

He nodded. "Don't hold that against me, though. I may work at the studio like any other relative, but I earn my pay."

We ankled back to the point where he'd rammed his sedan into the blonde twist's heap. I sprinkled some light in the roadster. Then I said: "Nuts!"

Young Hanley stared. "Something?"

I pointed. "You won't get her vital statistics from

the registration slip, after all."

"Why not?" his tone grew sharper than his beezer.

"This is a rented iron from one of the Hollywood U-drive agencies," I growled.

He swore; barged over to his Cad and opened its front door as if to climb in. All of a sudden he twitched like a guy who's been jabbed with a red-hot hypodermic. "Oh-h!" he yeeped. Then he started staggering around in circles, his steps as jerky as a mechanical toy.

I grabbed him. "What cooks?"

"The c-cans. The film. G-gone!"

"What film?"

He trembled. "The reels of my uncle's new costume p-production. The latest Supertone million dollar feature—"

"The one that was just previewed in Pasadena?"

He choked: "Y-yes. I was b-bringing the master print back to the studio. Twelve cans of spools. Somebody m-must have s-stolen them out of my car while we chased that girl!"

A hunch nipped me. "Looks to me as if you stepped into a frame, sonny."

"Frame?"

"Yeah. The yellow-haired doll probably doused her headlights and purposely drove in front of you, caused the accident. Then she deliberately lured you into trailing her afoot."

"You mean she had an accomplice waiting here to

steal the film as soon as she drew me away?"

"It makes sense," I said.

"No it doesn't," he stuck a gasper in his yap but forgot to light it. "It's preposterous!"

"Why is it?"

"Because in the first place, who'd know I was carrying those reels in my car? And in the second place, the original negative of the feature is in our film vaults out at the Supertone lot in Culver City. Nobody could possibly gain anything by stealing one positive master print. There'll be hundreds more prints made from the negative when the pic is released for distribution."

I said: "So okay. Maybe some dope just craved a souvenir of Hollywood."

About that time another car drew up, a limousine this trip. A Pasadena motorcycle cop also arrived. From the limousine bounced Ben Hanley, the little punk's uncle. He and the cop went into a questions-and-answers act with the harried nephew in the middle of a barrage of words and phrases.

I left them jawing there. If Spence Hanley wanted me for a witness he could contact me later. I drove home.

ABOUT nine o'clock the following morning a phone call jingled me awake. I reached out of bed, uncradled the instrument and said: "Speak right up. You're paying for it."

"Turner?"

"Yeah."

"You alone?"

"I am, although it's none of your business."

"Don't get your back hair in a kink. This is Duke Kinzer," the voice said.

I scowled. I knew Duke Kinzer—slightly. And what I knew about him I didn't like. He was a cheap two-bit grifter and penny ante louse around town, the kind of guy you prefer to see through a telescope. I said: "Sorry. He's out."

"Who's out?"

"Mr. Turner, suh. Dis-yere am de butler. Ah'll tell him y'all phoned him, yassuh. Goom-bye now."

Kinzer's tone hardened. "Cut out the ribbing, Sherlock. I got a proposition for you."

"Me velly slolly. Me-dumb Chinaboy, no spik-kada Ingleese. *Si, Senor,* I geeve your message to boss when he come een. I theenk thees weel be next year some time."

"Very funny," Kinzer said. "The dialect kills me. When I get done laughing, remind me to tell you I got a ten-grand melon I can cut with you. Fifty-fifty."

"Your melons are all sour, pal," I said. "I'm not interested."

"Maybe you'd be interested in this one. It's a cinch. A sure thing. Look. You'll be called in on a case out at Supertone some time today." He slid into a fast-talking whisper. "You can solve this case with the information I'm gonna give you. You can tap old Ben Hanley for at least ten G's reward dough. All I want is five thousand for myself"

In spite of my dislike for the Kinzer rodent, I decided to give his deal a smell—at least until I found out what it was. After all, I'm in the private snooping racket for all the geetus I can collect. "What's the case I'm to be called on?" I asked him. "And what information are you going to slip me?"

"Can't tell you now, Hawkshaw. But I'll ring you at your office right after lunch." He hung up.

I torched a wheezer, had an eye-opener of Vat 69, dunked my chassis in the shower and was piling into a set of threads when the phone rang again. I answered it.

The guy on the other end of the line crackled with excitement. "Turner? This is Ben Hanley of Supertone. I need you right away on an important matter. Can you come right over to Culver City and see me?"

"I'm practically half-way there this instant," I told him. I hung up, started to turn around—and felt the muzzle of a roscoe poking me in the left kidney.

"You won't go anywhere for a while," a she-male voice informed me quietly.

I PIVOTED; nearly swallowed my coffin-nail, fire and all. A young, blonde quail was standing close to me with her .25 automatic cocked and primed. It wasn't the roscoe that startled me, though. You get used to things like that in my business. What got me down was the jane herself.

She was the party who'd driven her rented roadster in front of young Spence Hanley's sedan the previous night and then made her getaway in the fog!

I hung the stupefied glimpse on her. "How did you get in my stash, Bright-Eyes?"

"Maybe I picked the lock. Maybe I bribed the janitor for a key. Maybe I came in the fire-escape window. Do you care?"

"I'm delighted. Or I would be if you'd put away that hog-leg. You're just what a bachelor apartment needs."

A SCORNFUL grin quirked her crimson lips. "So, a wise guy?"

"Wise enough to know a looker when I see one."

"Then you can get a good look while I'm driving you down to Manhattan Beach."

I said: "So we're going on a party, hunh?"

"Call it a vacation. There's a cozy little cabin all prepared for you. A nice week-end spot."

"I can't afford vacations, babe. Let's not go. Let's just stay here and have fun in Hollywood. They call me 'Tumbling Turner', 'cause I fall for anything wearing skirts."

"Lay a hand on me and I'll plug a hole in you, Sherlock," she warned me.

I doubted that. She didn't look like the type who'd actually pull the trigger on you for making a pass. She was delishfully streamlined in a tight frock; there was a cute tilt to her nose, a come-hither glint she couldn't keep out of her optics, and her complexion hadn't originated in a jar of cosmetics. Her hair was genuinely yellow without benefit of peroxide and her perfume smelled nice.

"You going to spend this vacation with me, hon?" I said.

"I am not."

I said: "In that case I won't go." I made a loose fist, brought it around in a half-circle and swatted her on the wrist. Her rod went clattering across the room and she let out a startled yeep. "Quiet," I snarled, and doled her a belt on the mush.

She went backward, lost her balance, toppled.

I followed it up by catching both her slender wrists in my left hand. Her blue glims shot sparks. "Stop it . . . let me g- go!"

"Cork it, sister. Before I give you another taste of my knuckles." As I pinioned her, I reached for a spare necktie on my dresser, knotted the jessie's arms behind her.

"Wh-what are you g-going to do?" she panted.

"Leave you here while I make a hurry-up visit to Culver City," I leered at her. "Then I'll come back and give your little trip to Manhattan Beach some more thought."

"You c-can't make me stay!" She was twisting, trying hard to get her wrists loose.

"I can try." I leaned down, looped another necktie around her ankles, drew it tight, tossed her onto my divan. Even then, I was afraid she might work her way loose, so I went to a bureau drawer, got out a bed-sheet, made long a strips of it and wrapped her like an Egyptian mummy. I shoved a gag in her mouth; and then, for good measure, I put a blanket over her and pinned the edges of the blanket to the divan with safety pins.

"So-long, Toots," I said, and ankled out.

BEN HANLEY was waiting for me in his lavish private sanctum on the Supertone lot. He was a fussy little blister with a bald dome fringed by wisps of grey hair, and his trumpet was even sharper than his nephew's. The nephew himself, Spence Hanley, was also in the office, jittery as a jockey at the start of the Kentucky Derby. And there was a third guy sitting in the room, a tall, skinny character dressed in black like an undertaker. He sneered at me as I barged in.

I sneered right back at him with compound interest. His name was Mortimer Wolf and he was president of Terrastar Productions—a rival studio. There'd been bad blood between Supertone and Terrastar for a long time, and I wondered what Wolf was doing in the enemy camp. His presence irked me for no especial reason. I just didn't go for the guy, was all.

Old Man Hanley said: "Thanks for coming, Turner. I'm in terrible trouble. The film of my latest super picture has b-been stolen."

"Yeah, I know. I was on deck when the reels were glommed out of Spence's sedan. But you've still got the negative."

The nephew started pacing up and down. "That's just it! Somebody broke into Uncle Ben's film vaults last night and made away with that negative. It must have happened around the same time the master positive was being taken from my Cadillac!"

"You mean you can't duplicate the print?"

"No," the punk's uncle gibbered. "A million dollar production—gone! We just finished the last takes a few days ago. Most of the sets are partly dismantled already. Some of the cast have been signed by other lots. The rushes were okayed, the necessary retakes made, and the cutters were all through editing and titling. You know that if you saw the preview last night. And now we got nothing to show for it! No negative, no master print—"

I caught my breath. The idea of purloining a million-buck movie was a brand new gag. I'd never heard of such a audacious stunt; but you had to admit the idea was tops. It had the earmarks of genius.

"Any suspicions?" I asked.

Ben Hanley shook his bald noggin. "No. But a man came in to see me this morning. He claimed to represent the ones who stole the film. He demanded a hundred thousand dollars for the return of the reels."

"A hundred grand?" I let out a low whistle.

"Yes. And I can't pay it. A hundred thousand would wipe out every dime in our treasury at the moment—and we need the money to pay Mr. Wolf, here," he gestured toward the tall, skinny president of the rival Terrastar outfit.

"How-come you owe Wolf that much scratch?"

"We're in a hole, Turner. We've had some flops recently. We hoped this new costume epic would pull us out. Otherwise—well, Mr. Wolf bought up a lot of our notes at the bank, and there's a payment due tomorrow. A quarter of a million, actually, but he's willing to accept a hundred thousand on account."

"A hundred thousand. No less, though," the Terrastar mogul grunted from somewhere down around his shoelaces. He reminded me of a cheap undertaker waiting for a sick man to kick the bucket. "I want the money or I'll put this studio in bankruptcy."

I looked him over. "But if you insist on your payment, Ben Hanley won't be able to buy back his feature."

"That's his lookout."

"Wait. If he uses what money he has to get his film back, he can probably make enough profit off it to satisfy your debt in full. Why don't you give him an extension?"

Wolf smiled. It was an unpleasant smile. "No extension. With me, money talks."

I SAID: "Yeah. It talks. It also stinks. You've got Hanley on the hook. No matter which way he wriggles, he's a gone goose. If he pays you, he can't buy back his stolen feature—so he goes bankrupt. If he buys it back, he can't pay you right away—so you put him in bankruptcy. He can't win."

"Are you accusing me of engineering the theft of his production, gumshoe?" Mortimer Wolf crossed one bony leg over the other and hung the sardonic focus on me.

"Not exactly. It's a theory, though."

"It's a lousy theory; my friend. I'm not trying to

wreck Supertone. I'm just protecting my own financial investments."

"That's nice," I said. "But of course if Supertone should go into receivership, you might buy it and merge it with Terrastar. Two companies for the price of one. It'd be a swell deal—for a mugg like you."

He shrugged. "Okay, so I'm a mugg. So I'm the mugg who suggested calling you in on the case. You're an appreciative louse, I must say."

I wanted to paste him but I restrained the impulse. There was a chance that he might be leveling; I had no way of knowing for sure—as yet. So I ignored him and swung back to Ben Hanley, who was plucking at the tufts of grey fuzz around his bald sconce: I said: "You're hiring me to locate the missing reels?"

"If that's possible."

"What about the guy that contacted you this morning? The one who demanded a hundred grand ransom for the film?"

"He said he was representing the parties who have the reels. He gave his own name as Duke Kinzer."

I jumped about seven inches straight up in the air. "Kinzer? Well, I'll be a—!"

Hanley's jockey-size nephew said: "What's the matter, Turner? Why does Kinzer's name startle you?"

"Because he phoned me this morning." Then I snapped my fingers. "I think I savvy the setup now! Kinzer is evidently on the verge of double-crossing his associates and selling out to me for a mere ten thousand plasters. He told me he'd call me again, right after lunch. Maybe I can pull your fat out of the fire after all."

As I said this, I was watching Mortimer Wolf from the tail of my peeper. He scowled, wrinkled his map as if he'd just chewed an unripe persimmon. "You really think so?" he said.

"I do indeed. And by the way, did any of you guys spill that you intended to hire me?"

Hanley quit worrying his tufts of hair. "Why, no. Not as far as I know. Nobody knew it except Mr. Wolf and my nephew and myself. What makes you think—?"

"It leaked out just the same," I snapped. "A blonde cutie came into my igloo a while ago; tried to stop me from coming here."

"A blonde—?" Young Spence goggled at me.

"Yeah, chum. The same one that ran her jalopy in front of yours last night."

"Good Lord!" the punk whispered. "What did she want?"

"I didn't take time to ask her. I was in a hurry. She'll keep, though. I left her tied up. So now I'm going back to beat some information out of her while I'm waiting for Duke Kinzer's phone call." And I ankled out, conscious of three pairs of eyes following me, speculating, wondering . . .

When I got to my parked coupe I took a swivel around; didn't pipe anybody watching me. So I leaned down, let all the ozone out of my left hind tire. As soon as it was flat, I hunted up a parking lot attendant; killed ten minutes helping him change over to my precious spare.

Presently I got rolling in the direction of my wig-wam; took my time. Sure enough, when I got there and peered into my apartment, the blonde doll was gone.

SOMEBODY had sliced open the blanket that pinned her down; had cut the strips of sheet that bound her like a bandage. Then she'd powdered.

There was a grin on my kisser, which I lubricated with a shot of Scotch. Everything had worked out exactly as I'd foreseen; and the wren's lam bore out certain suspicions that were taking shape in my think-tank. So now my next move would be to put the finger on Duke Kinzer. Once I located him, I figured to clear up the mess in short order.

I drove to certain apartments where the rat had lived at one time or another, but I threw snake-eyes every time. Kinzer moved oftener than a Mexican jumping bean with the hotfoot—frequently without paying his overdue rent. And he always carefully avoided leaving any forwarding address. Afraid his former landladies might catch up with him, was the way I doped it.

One wise old dame of an apartment manager disputed this, however. She told me: "Don't be silly, young man. He wasn't afraid of landladies. He was afraid of those waitresses he runs around with. One of them's probably looking for him with a marriage license in one hand and a shotgun in the other."

I could have kissed the old bag. She handed me the tip I should have remembered for myself—Kinzer's weakness for hash house she-males. I thanked her and hied myself to a cheap beanery on lower Hollywood Boulevard where a dish by the name of Mae Hainey dealt 'em off the arm. I'd seen her in Kinzer's company on several occasions, and maybe she could spot him for me.

Not that I expected her to push out any voluntary information. But I had a scheme to get it out of her.

For once in my life, I got a break when I barged into the eatery. It was just time for the shift of waitresses to change, and the Hainey cupcake was back of the counter taking off her apron, perching a screwy hat on her henna-red tresses. I turned, blipped back to the sidewalk, waited until she came out. Then I fell into step with her.

"Hi, sweet stuff. Your name Hainey? Mae Hainey?"

She gave me the sidewise swivel. "Blow, big boy. Whatever it is you're sellin', that's what it is I ain't buyin'."

"That's too bad, hon. I'm not selling anything except maybe a few drinks. For free."

She lifted a rouged lip. "Drinks at this time in the morning? You must work on the swing shift somewhere. Go on, cousin, scram."

"Okay. So I'll scram. So I'll give Duke what-for."

"Duke who?"

"Kinzer. He gave me your name, told me you were a good kid—to look you up. I just got in from Seattle, and—"

"Duke Kinzer told you—?"

"Don't get him wrong, baby. Don't get me wrong, either. Duke just told me that if I was lonesome, I should drop in at the beanery and say hello."

"Well, Duke better not talk around about me—"

I said: "Skip it. I made a mistake, is all. I wanted somebody to have some drinks with me and maybe go to a show or something. Can't a lonesome guy look for company in a strange town? Well, thanks anyhow." I started to haul hips in the opposite direction.

SHE nailed me by the arm, pulled me back. "Don't be in such a rush. Maybe I'm lonesome too. Only I don't like guys to think they can pick me up like I was a tramp. Not strange guys, anyhow. I'm a lady, I'll have you know. And my old woman was a lady before me."

"Sure, hon, sure," I said. "Anybody can see you've got breeding." Actually, standing on the corner with her made me feel as conspicuous as a wop selling balloons at the Ritz.

She said sullenly: "Buy me a drink?"

"That was the general idea when I first started," I told her. There was a cocktail dispensary handy and I steered her into its dim depths. The joint smelled of stale beer. We took a rear booth and gave the bar-keep our orders. He brought them. Vat 69 for me and a double rye for Mae. She tossed it off neat with a chaser of beer. Then she had another of the same.

After the third prescription, she said confidentially: "Funny thing about me. Whiskey never affects me."

"Really?"

"But beer. I can feel that stuff t-the minute it hits bottom. I feel it now. Makes me warm." She got up from across the table and slid into the booth on my bench. "You feel the stuff handsome?"

"I do now," I slid an arm around her waist, drew her nearer. "It isn't just the drink, either. It's you."

She giggled gravely. "I think you're cute. Wanna kiss?"

I told her yes, which was a complete lie, and pressed my mouth to hers. "Oh, boy!"

"Whatsamatter, honey?" She giggled. "You're cute. I like you. Gotta tell Duke how nice you are."

"Not today you won't," I said. "Not when his leg

hurts so bad."

"Whose leg?"

"Duke's. Duke Kinzer's. The left one."

"It didn't hurt him last night," she said. "The right one either. You kidding me?"

I looked at her. "You mean you haven't heard what happened to him this morning? What happened to his leg, I mean?"

"No. What happened to it?"

"He busted it." I picked up a burned match, snapped it by way of illustration. "Fell down a manhole."

SHE stood up suddenly. "Duke should of called me. Gonna go see him. What hospital is he at?"

"No hospital. Home."

"You got a car?"

"Sure."

"Take me there."

I paid my bill and we went out of the groggery to my bucket at the curb. As I helped her in, I pretended to stumble. "Ouch! I've sprained my ankle and can't drive."

"So gimme your key." Which was just what I was hoping she'd say. Now she would take me to Kinzer and I didn't even have to ask her for his address.

There would be trouble, though, when she found out his stem wasn't really broken. En route, I figured out an answer to this. And when we finally reached the door of his apartment in a shabby stash north of Franklin, I put my scheme to work; made a regretful fist and pasted the red-haired bim on the dimple.

It was a dirty trick but I was forced to it. I caught her as she sagged, toted her to a broom closet farther along the corridor and stowed her with the mops and vacuum cleaners. Then I belted back to Duke's portal; knocked.

Nobody answered. I tried the knob but it was locked. I hauled forth my ring of master keys, found one that operated the latch; let myself in. And then, as I crossed the threshold, an ugly sensation slugged me in the pit of the elly-bay with the force of a battering ram. I whispered: "What the—?"

Duke Kinzer was strewn on the threadbare carpet with a hole in his head; a bullet hole. He was deader than Confederate money.

HE HADN'T been defunct more than ten or fifteen minutes; his wrist was still limber, faintly warm. I'd missed his killer by just that short a time—and I realized Duke had been bumped off by his boss in the Supertone feature-film theft. The shootery had been committed on account of this unknown boss finding out that Kinzer was planning a double-cross: had figured to sell out to me for a lousy fifty-fifty split of ten grand instead of waiting to collect the whole hundred thousand.

And there were just three guys who knew about

Duke's phone call to me. They knew because I'd told them. They were Ben Hanley of Supertone, his nephew Spence, and Mortimer Wolf from the Terrastar outfit.

Frankly, I wasn't sure which one of them was the guilty character. But I was beginning to have a slim idea, along with an even slimmer chance of collaring the bozo in question. It would all depend on a certain loose parcel in my jalopy. I straightened up, made for the door

It opened in my face and Mae Hainey lurched in. Her peepers were glassy, there was a mouse under her kisser where I'd bopped her, and she had a mop handle in her mitts from the broom closet I'd forgotten to lock when I stuffed her there. She swung the mop handle like a niblick; teed off on my noggin before I had a chance to duck.

She scored par. I went bye-bye.


I WOKE up to the rhythmic tune of somebody slapping me across the chops with his open palm. When I opened my blinkers, I stared into the beefy lineaments of my friend Dave Donaldson, homicide squad lieutenant. The room was infested with his minions, and two guys were lugging Duke Kinzer's remainders out of the joint in a wicker meat-basket.

Donaldson snarled: "Okay, Sherlock. Start belching before I kick the truth out of you."

I sat up groggily, jabbed my thumbs at his eyeballs to drive him off me. "Desist," I grunted. "You know well enough I didn't chill the guy."

"This lady says you did. She put in the bleat to headquarters and told us." He gestured toward the Hainey jane.

I said: "She made a mistake. And she's no lady."

That drew fire from the redhead. "By gosh, I'm more of a lady I than you are, you stinkin' son! I'll—"

A couple of harness bulls grabbed her, held her. I staggered to my pins, fastened the clutch on Donaldson's elbow. "Come with me. Maybe I can clean up this mess for you."

"Oh, yeah? How?"

"You'll see. Come on, get moving." And I dragged him out of the igloo, took him into my coupe. Then I produced the parcel I'd been hankering to examine. It was the little leather purse I'd glommed from the golden-haired cutie in my apartment that morning—the wren who had later lammed with the help of somebody else.

Dave hung the hinge on it. "What goes on?"

"This," I said, and opened the catch. I frisked inside; found a driver's license. It was made out to one Norah Doran and the address was a bungalow court just off Wilshire.

"Well?" Dave asked me grimly.

I said: "Maybe good, maybe bad. We've got to make knots." We piled into my heap and I souped the cylinders. On the way, I explained my theories.

Presently I parked a block away from my destination; argued Dave into playing ball with me. He protested but finally caved in; followed me at a discreet distance as I barged toward the bungalow court.

When I was sure he was out of view, I went to the rear cottage, thumbed the bell, dragged my .32 automatic from the armpit holster where I always carry it for emergencies. In a moment the bungalow door opened and I was face to face with the golden-haired dame who'd run her roadster in front of Spence Hanley's sedan last night.

"Norah Doran?"

"Yes. Oh-h-h. . . it's y-you . . .!"

I put the muzzle of my rod against her frightened puss. "One yeep and it gives bullets for lunch, baby," I said. Then I pushed her backward into the wigwam; followed her.


THERE were a lot of Gladstone bags and miscellaneous luggage scattered around the wikiup, some packed, some waiting for cargo. I said: "Getting ready to take it on the lam, eh, hon?"

"What's it to you? You can't b-break in here and—"

"Guess again, sweet stuff. I'm hep to the whole setup. And unless you turn state's evidence, you're going to find your gorgeous form resting on a cold hard bench in the gow."

"I d-don't know what you me-mean!"

I gave her a pleasant leer. "So I'll explain. You and

your boy friend stewed up a slick trick to garner a quick hundred G's. The idea was to swipe a million buck Supertone opus and hold it for ransom. Duke Kinzer was hired to help."

Her breathing got gusty.

"You—you!"

I said: "First your sweetie took the negative reels from the Supertone vaults; an inside job. Then, last night, you drove a rented roadster in front of Spence Hanley's chariot. And when Spence gave chase, Duke Kinzer was on the job to steal the only existing positive-print spools."

"Prove it!"

I ignored this. "Then Kinzer became the contact guy; the go-between. He delivered your demand for a hundred thousand fish as the price of the feature's return. However, he apparently got sore at you for some reason; maybe because you weren't cutting him in for a big enough slice of the take. So he tried to cross you by phoning me, offering to sell out for five thousand."

She was a little more composed, now. "This is all Greek to me, bub."

"Yeah, but I'm translating it for you. When Kinzer phoned me, it was a tip-off. How could he know in advance that I was going to be called in on the case? He must have been close to somebody who told him. And only three guys were aware that I was to be hired: Ben Hanley, his nephew, and Mortimer

Wolf."

"Well?"

"So it had to be one of those three who'd glommed the production. I proved this to my own satisfaction by telling all of them that I had you locked in my stash and then allowing enough time for the guilty party to rescue you. Unfortunately, though, I allowed too much time. Because after your boy friend released you from my dugout, he did something else."

"Something . . . else?"

"Something that'll buy him a one-way ticket to the smoke house at San Quentin," I nodded. "He bumped Duke Kinzer."

All the starch went out of her. She swayed against me, clung like a frightened mustard-plaster. "I . . . I didn't know there'd be a m-murder! I swear I didn't! oh-h-h, please . . . Don't let me be involved! Take me away! I'll . . . pay you . . ."

I said: "Maybe we can make a deal if you'll tell me your sweetie's name, hon."

She started to say something but never got it out. That was because a roscoe started sneezing from the kitchen doorway. It spewed: *Ka-chow! Chow!* and the blonde quail stiffened, twitched convulsively. Then she went very limp. Who wouldn't go limp with a pair of slugs in her cranium?

I dropped her; catapulted at the kitchen with my own gat set to spray lead all over the precinct. Then

I heard a frightful commotion in the back yard.
Dave Donaldson's voice roared: "Got you, rat!"

WHEN I reached the rear doorway, he was macing
Ben Hanley over the bald spot with one hand and
putting the nippers on the old blister's wrists with
the other. Hanley was caterwauling like a wildcat
with its tail in a crack; and his smoking cannon lay at
his feet where Dave had knocked it.

I said: "Nice work, chum. He just browned Norah
Doran with that howitzer. And I'll bet my last dollar
it'll match up with the slug that chilled Duke Kinzer,
too."

"What's the difference? We can only gas him
once."

I hung the focus on the Hanley bozo. "It had to be
you," I told him. "The theft of the negative from
your vaults was an inside job, which eliminated
Mortimer Wolf. So it rested between you and your
nephew. But Spence practically cleared himself
when the positive print was taken from his Cad sedan. He was shocked, but not too worried. He
pointed out that more prints could be made—which
indicated he knew nothing about the negative being
swiped."

"Blast you!" the old guy tore hunks of grey tuft
from the fringe around his shiny noggin.

I said: "Your studio was about bankrupt. And this
million dollar costume opus was a turkey. It stunk. It

wouldn't draw flies at the box office. So you figured to steal it and buy it back for the last hundred grand in your treasury—paying the dough to yourself, actually. That would clean out Supertone's coffers and Mortimer Wolf would take over; but at least you'd have a hundred thousand dollars saved from the deal. It might have worked, too, if you hadn't gone murder-haywire."

He started to curse me. Then all of a sudden his puss turned pasty and he clutched at his shirt-front. Heart disease, the doctors said at the autopsy. All I know is, Hanley was deceased before he hit the ground with his profile.

Later I found the missing cans of film in the late lamented Nora Doran's bungalow; turned them over to young Spence Hanley, who inherited the Supertone lot. Mortimer Wolf gambled some more financing on the jockey-sized punk, and between them they remade the costume opus—salvaged parts of it and re-shot the rest. It turned out to be a click all over the country.

I drew a fee of five thousand clams and spent part of it on a roaring binge with the red-haired waitress, Mae Hainey. Maybe she wasn't a lady, but sometimes you get tired of ladies.

# SHAKEDOWN SHAM

"I think my wife is being blackmailed," the guy opened up. And Dan agreed to protect the dame while she kept her secret tryst. It wasn't until after she'd kept her clandestine appointment that he had a real idea of how big a job he'd taken upon himself

T HE GUY helped himself to a gasper from the pack on my desk and said: "I think my wife is being blackmailed, Mr. Turner. I want you to look into it."

I leaned forward with a lighted match; put the focus on him as I furnished fire for the coffin-nail in his handsome mouth. His name was Toby Vaughan. he'd been an All American football fullback a few years ago, and he still had the appearance of a gridiron hero. His frame was big, muscular; his skin had a tan outdoors freshness to match the competent slant of threads that had cost plenty of scratch.

He hadn't bought those clothes out of his movie salary, however. I knew enough about him to savvy that much. Ever since his college days he'd been hanging around the various lots, playing bit roles and extra parts in mob scenes, waiting for the break that never came. He just happened to be one of those good looking but unfortunate lugs with an amiable disposition, an ambitious nature and not an ounce of acting ability. Characters of his kidney are a dime a dozen in Hollywood, and you can't help feeling sorry for them as a class.

IN Toby Vaughan's case, though, your sympathy would be wasted. His wife was the former Kay Holliston, an Oklahoma oil heiress with more dough than a pickle has warts. They'd been married maybe a year, give or take a month; and from a financial standpoint Vaughan was even better off than if he'd had a starring contract with the biggest studio in town.

Moreover, the gossip-mongers said the marriage was a genuine love match; and I was inclined to believe this when I piped the worried expression on Toby's face. He figured his frau was in a jackpot of some sort, and he wanted to get her out of it. Otherwise he wouldn't be seeking the services of a private ferret.

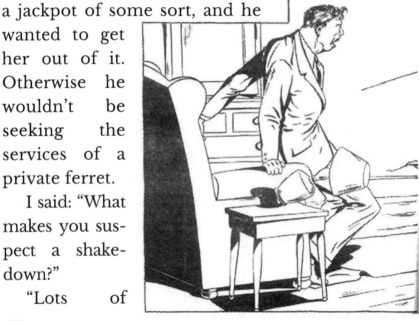

I said: "What makes you suspect a shakedown?"

"Lots of

things. None of them conclusive, perhaps; but when they're all added together they look ugly."

"List them for me," I suggested.

He dragged on his butt. "Well, to start with, Kay's income has been hit pretty hard by the gasoline rationing program. Her money's in oil property, you understand; independent producing and refining companies, service stations, and so forth. You know

what the war has done to the petroleum industry."

"Yeah," I said "Motorists with 'A' cards aren't buying much

ethyl."

"Exactly. As a result, Kay's liquid cash isn't what it might be. And in the past couple of months there's been a mysterious drain on it. She's withdrawn close to a hundred and fifty thousand dollars I can't account for unless it's because she's being bled white."

"Is that your only reason for suspecting blackmail?"

He reached in his pocket. "No. I found the torn pieces of a note in her waste basket this morning. Perhaps it wasn't ethical, but I put them together and read them. Here, see for yourself." And he handed me a sheet of paper to which he'd pasted a series of scraps, like a jigsaw puzzle.

I copped a swivel at the typewritten message:

*"Mrs. Vaughan*
*Meet me at five P. M. Tuesday, room 607, Constantine Hotel. Bring ten thousand cash, no new bills. This time I guarantee to give you what you want.*

*He Who Knows"*

"Looks as if you're right about the shakedown angle," I said. I gave him back the letter and added: "Do you think she'll keep the appointment? Today's Tuesday."

Vaughan made a bitter mouth. "I'm sure she'll go. I followed her to the bank this morning; saw her draw out ten thousand dollars in old currency. And then I shadowed her to a Main Street pawn shop. She bought a gun; a second-hand automatic."

I said: "Oh-oh! That's not so good.'

"You're right it's not," he growled. "That's why I've come to you. I don't want to appear in the thing personally; I'd prefer not to have her learn that I've found out about the affair. You see, I—I care for her too much to have anything come between us. No matter what she's done to fall into the hands of a blackmailer, she mustn't know I'm aware of it."

"And what would you like me to do?" I asked him.

"Go to the Constantine. Take Room 609, next to 607. If—if anything happens, I want Kay protected at all costs." He stripped a century out of his wallet, passed it to me. "Is this enough for an advance retainer?"

"Yeah, if it's all you can spare," I said. "It may cost you more, though, before we're finished. We can discuss that later." I stood up, ushered him out of the office.

AT FOUR o'clock that afternoon I parked my jalopy around the corner from the Constantine Hotel, barged into the joint's shabby lobby and ankled over to a desk clerk who needed a haircut and shave. He stopped studying a Racing Form long enough to ask me if I wanted something.

"Yeah. A room," I said.

He looked for luggage; saw I didn't have any.

"Our rates—" he started to say.

I tossed him a ten spot. "Sure, I know. In advance. Take out a day's rent and keep the change for yourself. Put it on Kayak's nose in the fifth at Tanforan; win yourself a yacht. That is, if I can have 609."

"Certainly sir. Thank you very much, sir. 609, you wanted? Let's see. Yes, it's vacant. Register right here. Boy! Now where is that bell-hop? Never mind, I'll take you up myself. Follow me, sir."

Instead of my real monicker I signed the book John Jones; then I tailed the guy to the elevator and presently found myself in the room I'd requested. As soon as the clerk was gone, I locked the portal, then gumshoed over to the connecting door between my quarters and the adjoining 607. I put my ear to the panel; listened, but didn't hear anything. Evidently there was nobody home in there.

This was just dandy. I pulled my penknife, opened a special blade designed for boring holes in woodwork; reamed an imperceptible peep-hole in the portal eye level. When I applied my glimmer to the result, I could lamp a fairly large area of that adjacent chamber.

I waited.

At a quarter to five somebody came into 607; a sallow, furtive little jerk with a receding chin and buck teeth that gave him the appearance of a hungry squirrel. He sat down on a chair, twitching like a hophead.

I kept on waiting.

AT FIVE sharp there was a faint knock on the door of the room occupied by Squirrel-Puss. He got up, answered it, and I copped a hinge at Toby Vaughan's wife. The instant I piped her, my temperature soared for the higher brackets.

She was a lot prettier than her newspaper pictures indicated. Her hair was the color of sunlight; not golden, not copper, but bright as a morning on the desert. Her map was clear, chiseled, and she wore a pale blue dress that adhered to her like sprayed paint.

She faced the sallow jerk. "You have the letters?"

"Let's see the dough first, babe," he said.

She opened her big blue leather handbag; rummaged out a wad of geetus. "Here."

"You don't mind if I count it, do you?" Squirrel-Puss snatched the cabbage, leafed through it. Presently he stowed it away in a worn wallet, returned the wallet to his inside coat pocket and gave vent to a soapy chuckle. "Ten G's. Thanks, hon."

"The letters, please," the Vaughan quail's voice trembled on the thin edge of hysteria.

Squirrel-Puss said: "Now, ain't that just too bad, sweetness? You know I hate to disappoint you, but, when I went to get them letters from my safety deposit box, I was just five minutes late. The bank had closed."

"You lie!"

"Is that a way to talk? I wouldn't kid you, sis. Can a guy get into a bank when it's closed? Sure not. So I guess you'll have to wait until next time. I'll drop you a line when I need another payoff; then we'll do business."

Kay Vaughan sucked in a quavery breath. At the same instant she delved into her handbag again; produced a pearl-handled .28 roscoe.

"There isn't going to be another payoff," she whispered tautly. "This is the last one. *This is it.*"

Squirrel-Puss let out a bleating yeep. "Hey, nix! Don't aim that thing at me! Please, don't!"

Watching through the hole in the door, I tabbed the tension on her beautiful mush; saw her finger tighten on the gat's trigger. I gasped: "What the —!" as I realized I couldn't prevent what was about to happen. The blonde doll was lined up dead ferninst me with the little jerk frozen before her. . .

The .28 sneezed *Ka-Chowp!* in a sharp staccato, its report so hemmed in by the room's walls that it seemed to have a heavier echo. Squirrel-Puss staggered, clawed at his skinny bellows; folded like a wet paper bag.

I GATHERED my hundred and ninety pounds of heft, smashed at the thin portal so hard I rammed it off its hinges in a shower of toothpicks. My left shoulder throbbed like an ulcerated tooth as I catapulted over the threshold.

"Now, then," I said, hoping against hope there would be no more fireworks and realizing I had to use strategy to keep any further murders from taking place.

The Vaughan chick stared at me. "Wh-who— how—?"

I snapped: "Belay the questions," and wrenched the rod out of her slender fingers; stowed it in my pocket while I risked hunkering down by the fallen jerk to inspect the tunnel in his ticker.

"Is—is he—?"

"Yeah," I said. "Deader than democracy in Berlin." I delved for the guy's wallet; got it. I also got a smear of ketchup on my mitt, which I wiped on the defunct bozo's shirt. He didn't mind; laundry bills weren't worrying him from now on.

There wasn't anything in the wallet except the lettuce which Kay Vaughan had just paid out; nothing to identify the blackmailer. I took a squint at the greenbacks, put them back, replaced the bill-fold where I'd found it. Then I straightened up, slipped an arm around the yellow-haired doll's pliant waist. For her protection I had to get her out of there instead of making the investigation I really wanted to make. "Let's go."

"N-no! Turn me loose! I—I must call the po-police and tell them I've k-killed a man!"

I hauled her toward the next room. "Stew the

cops. I'll notify them when the time comes. Right now we're powdering before anything else happens." I steered her through 609 to the corridor; peered out. The hall looked deserted, which was a nice break for our side. I nudged the shivering filly to a rear staircase and we slipped downward.

At the main floor I slowed to a casual walk; made her do the same. We sauntered through the shoddy lobby, gained the street; whereupon she turned her pallid puss toward me and halted in her tracks.

"I tell you I've g-got to give myself up! Don't you understand I'm a—a m-murderess?"

"I understand plenty, hon."

"If you don't let me go, I'll scream!"

I said quietly: "Okay. If you're so set on going down to the gow I'll accommodate you. Here's my coupe; I'll run you to headquarters. Climb aboard."

She obeyed, and I turned my attention to the job of driving.

I used my right hand for steering purposes because my left arm ached to beat hell. Smashing into the door between the two hotel rooms hadn't done my shoulder any good, although at the moment I couldn't estimate the amount of damage; sometimes a surface injury hurts worse than the deep kind.

The cupcake with the sunshine coiffure said: "Wh-where are you going? This isn't the w-way to police headquarters!"

"Cork the chatter, hon. I'm running this show," I

told her. And a little later I drew up before my own apartment stash, parked and got out. "Come along."

She hung the puzzled glimpse on me. "Wh-what's the meaning of th-this? Where are we?" Her voice was thin, frightened.

"You'll find out. Quit wasting time." I pulled her to the sidewalk and she took a harried gander up

and down the street in the gathering dusk. There was nobody in sight as she tried to get free of my grasp.

"I—I don't understand—" she whimpered.

I said: "Who cares?" and prodded her inside the building. We entered the automatic elevator arid I poked the "3" button. Pretty soon we were in my igloo. I locked the door, put the key in my pants and switched on the lights.

She stared at me again. "This is almost like—like a kidnaping!"

"Something of the sort, sweet stuff."

"But—but can't you realize I've k-killed a man? I've got to g-give myself up!"

"Not yet a while, you don't," I growled. "I have other plans for you. They don't include your going to the jug."

"You can't stop me!" she made a dig toward the door.

I SAID: "That's what you think," and pinioned her. "You're staying right here until I give you the office to scram. And you can have your choice of being quiet about it or taking a poke on the button."

She tried to pull away. "No—you mustn't—I won't let you t-touch me—" I indicated my bedroom. "Go in there and strip off your duds."

*"No!"*

"Hurry up. You can pass your clothes to me. I

promise not to peep."

"You—you mean—?"

"I mean you've got me all wrong if you think this is about to become a necking party. That's not the idea at all."

"Then wh-what is the idea of asking me t-to . . . undress?"

I said: "So you won't take a notion to lam. When you're peeled down to your underthings, stay put."

"But wh-why should I? Is it m-money you're after?"

"No. I could have taken that ten grand you paid to Squirrel-Puss," I reminded her. "Being deceased, he wouldn't have minded. But I didn't glom it, which ought to prove I'm neither a thief nor a blackmailer."

"What are you, then?"

"Just a dopey private ferret, is ail. Now get out of your garb or I'll do the job myself."

"You wouldn't dare!"

"Wouldn't I, though?" I reached toward her. It was a bluff—but it worked. She whimpered, ducked me, scuttled into the bedroom. A minute later her raiment began fluttering over the threshold to make a fragrant silken pile: the pale blue dress, sheer nylon hose and finally her spike-heeled patent pumps.

While she was still hidden from view, I gathered up her duds and toted them into the bathroom; locked them in a cabinet. At the same time I shucked my coat, took a squint at my throbbing shoulder and the patch of red on my shirt sleeve. It wasn't bad. I used some iodine, put my coat back on, ankled back to the living room.

The Vaughan cutie was standing there, wrapped in a bathrobe of mine and looking like a woeful blonde goddess. "Now wh-what?" she asked me dully.

"Just make yourself at home and keep your chin up, hon. Pretty soon everything's going to be jake." I powdered from the apartment.

DOWN at my office I dialed Toby Vaughan at his sumptuous wikiup in Westwood. Presently his clear voice came over the wire, worried, jittery. "Hello?"

"Dan Turner talking."

"Thank God, I've been waiting to hear from you! Where's my wife? What happened to her? Did you know a man was found d-dead in that hotel room at the Constantine?"

I said: "Yeah. Kay acted faster than I expected. She pulled a rod and blasted before I could smash in to stop her."

"But where is she? Do the police suspect—?"

"I don't know what they suspect," grunted. "As far as your wife is concerned, though, she's safe enough. Temporarily, anyhow. I may be able to get her out from under the rap—but it's going to cost you plenty."

"How much?"

"Say five grand for a starter."

"I—I'll send it right over to you. I can't come myself; I have a business engagement. But if you'll be in your office within the next half hour, I'll—"

I said: "I'll be here," and rang off. To kill time, I got a fresh fifth of Vat 69 from my desk and started working on it. Twenty minutes and four jorums later a messenger arrived, handed me an envelope, took a receipt, and beat it. I opened the envelope, extracted a wad of cabbage, counted it to make sure. Then I shuffled down to my jalopy, aimed for police headquarters.

My friend Dave Donaldson of the homicide squad was on deck when I got there. "Hi, chum," I said. "Why the apoplectic countenance?"

He gave me a glare that would have curdled vinegar. "You'd be apoplectic too if you had my troubles! I don't know why I don't retire and take up chicken farming or something. I got indigestion, dandruff, stomach ulcers, and a sinus infection; and then on top of that I run into a hotel kill that makes no more sense than a maniac counting pink hop-toads—"

"You're talking about that bump-off in Room 607 of the Constantine?" I asked him innocently.

He leaped six feet straight up in the air like a guy who'd been tickled by a length of barbed wire. "What do you know about that mess?" he caterwauled.

I said: "Plenty. Wait until I put through a phone call; then maybe I'll help you make the pinch."

His glims narrowed. "Say, chum! The desk clerk at the Constantine said he rented a room to some big bozo in tweeds just before the murder happened. He told me this big bozo asked for the room next door to where the corpse was found. He—"

"Did the big bozo register as John Jones?"

"Yeah, and the description fits you!"

I broke out a gasper, torched it. "Wouldn't it be funny if I turned out to be John Jones?" I grinned. Then I eluded his enraged grasp; ducked out to the corridor and wedged myself in a public phone booth. I dropped a jitney in the slot, dialed a columnist acquaintance of mine on the *Morning Post*; a newspaper skulk who knew everything about everybody.

PRESENTLY I made connections, asked a question, got the right answer. When I ankled out of the booth, I bounced full into Dave Donaldson's waiting embrace. He mauled me against the wall with his weight; shoved his mush close to mine.

"Now, then, Sherlock!" he snarled. "Suppose you tell me what goes on!"

"Sure, bub. Keep your blood pressure under control and let's take a little spin in your official chariot."

"Where to!"

I said: "The apartment igloo of a frail named Lucette Landon."

"And who is Lucette Landon?"

"Just a dame. Central Casting lists her as an extra on call whenever any of the studios need chorus wrens or dress-up fillies for society scenes," I told him casually.

He backed off; glued the suspicious glance on me. "You mean she's hooked in with that hotel croaking?"

"Sort of." I headed for the exit and Dave lumbered along at my heels, snorting to himself like a volcano craving to erupt all over the precinct.

We piled into his police sedan and he gunned the ball bearings out of it; headed for the address I gave him. Bye and bye we dragged anchor in front of a gaudy structure on Sunset, the kind where the monthly rental on a single room would cost you a young fortune.

Dave said: "Pretty expensive joint for an extra doll."

I nodded, made for the lobby, accosted the desk clerk. "Miss Lucette Landon in her stash, cousin?"

"Yes, sir. She went up about thirty minutes ago. I'll ring her for you. Name, please?"

I tossed him a five-spot. "Never mind. We'll go up without an announcement and surprise her. She alone?"

"At the moment, sir."

I made a gesture to Donaldson and he tailed me to the elevator. We got off at the fourth floor, came to the Landon quail's wigwam. Dave raised his knuckles to knock.

"Ix-nay," I whispered as I reached for my ring of master keys. "Let's do some snooping first."

He piped me trying various keys on the look. "Hey, this isn't legal! You want me to lose my badge for participating in a burglary?"

"Look the other way and you won't see me doing it," I advised him. Then, when I got the door open: "Come on—and no noise."

He mumbled in his gums, hesitated; followed me inside. I made a swift frisk of the layout without spotting anybody, although you could hear a shower splashing in the bathroom.

Satisfied, I found a closet and opened it.

Donaldson whispered: "What's that for?"

"It's where you're to hide. Get in and stay in until I signal for you. And pray my scheme works."

He told me he didn't know any prayers but he had a rabbit's foot he could rub. "I don't think it'll help, though," he added sourly. "Every time I try it in a dice game I throw craps."

"Then just keep your fingers crossed," I closed the closet door on him. Then I made for the bathroom; reached it just as something exceptionally gorgeous in a gossamer negligee was coming out. This delishful dish was a diminutive brunette with sparkling black peepers and more curves than the Burma Road.

I said: "Hi, Toots. Are you Lucette Landon?"

She gasped, whirled so fast that her kimono almost slipped its moorings. "Wh-who—what on earth—Say, what's the idea of sneaking in here this way? I'll give you just two seconds to get out of here before I scream for the cops!"

"Why bother, babe? I'm a cop myself, sort of," I flashed the tin pinned on my vest.

THE color leaked out of her piquant pan. "Is—is this—you mean it's a pinch?"

"That depends on what you're guilty of," I said. "Innocent people rarely get sent to the bastille."

"Then scram. I'm innocent," she tried to pull a bluster on me but it was strictly from corn; didn't register. "You haven't got a thing on me."

I gave her the fishy eye. "Are you sure?" I worked on her conscience.

"Certainly I'm sure."

"You haven't been taking blackmail dough?" I prodded her some more.

She drew a quavery breath. "So that's it."

"Yeah, hon. I'm afraid it is."

A speculative look came into her narrowed optics. "How much do you want for giving me a break, letting me get out of town before the blowoff? My bags are packed."

"I noticed them," I said. "Sorry, though. I'm not interested in bribery coin. What I'd rather catch is the rat you're planning to elope with."

"Me? Elope? What a laugh!"

"You're not expecting anybody?"

"Of course not."

"In that case . . ." I hauled her into my arms, swooped my kisser toward hers.

She began squirming, struggling. "Nix! Not here . . . not just now!" she panted. "Wait until. . . ."

From the doorway behind me a snarling voice said: "Wait until when, you two-timing tramp?" And then a heavy hand fell on my shoulder, yanked me backward off-balance. Somebody aimed a Sunday punch at my profile.

I staggered, ducked the newcomer's knuckles, righted myself and dug out my roscoe. *"Okay, Toby Vaughan. Freeze."* Then, as loud as I could bellow: *"Hey, Dave, come in and put the nippers on this rodent! He's the murderer!"*

THE GOOD looking, sun-tanned former football hero pivoted in his tracks. He was just in time to receipt for a bash on the button from Dave Donaldson. There was a metallic glitter, a click of steel, and Vaughan was wearing official police bracelets.

Then the brunette Landon chick yeeped again.

"Quiet, babe," I snapped at her. "So far, you're out

of this except maybe as an accessory; the recipient of the blackmail lettuce. So stow your screeches unless you yearn to accompany your sweetie to the gas chamber."

Toby Vaughan's chiseled puss turned six shades of pale. "Wh-what do you m-mean, gas chamber?"

I said: "You're the louse that committed killery on Squirrel-Face in Room 607 of the Constantine. You were hiding in a closet. You fired at the same instant your wife did; and it was your slug that bumped the little guy."

"Prove it!" he dared me.

I frisked him, lifted a heater from his hip pocket. "I'll make book the bullet in the sallow mug's ticker matches the rifling of this gat. That should be proof enough."

He went green around the fringes. "God—I forgot to toss the gun away—!" It was the same as a confession, and he seemed to realize it the minute the words spilled out of his yap. "How did you guess—?"

I said: "I didn't guess. I was sure of it. I cinched my suspicions when I phoned you, asked for five grand. The money you sent me came from the defunct jerk's wallet."

"Wh-what?"

"Yeah. I'd examined those green-backs when I inspected his remainders. I saw where some of his gravy had stained the bills. Those same stains were on the geetus you sent me; which meant you'd taken

it out of his pocket after I hauled your wife from the hotel."

Vaughan seemed to shrink in his tailored threads. "Smart, aren't you?"

"Sometimes," I admitted modestly. "The way I add it up, you were the one who'd been blackmailing Kay. You used Squirrel-Puss as a stooge. You'd finally glommed practically all of your frau's ready assets; then you decided to croak your go-between so he'd never spill. Moreover, you framed the kill so Kay would take the fall; which would keep your own skirts clear. That's why you hired me to watch from Room 609, so I'd be a witness when she apparently murdered the mug."

"Ridiculous!" he snarled. "You can't prove I was anywhere near the death room at the time of the shooting. If you'd thought so, why didn't you smoke me out instead of forcing Kay to leave with you?"

I said: "I had a good reason, bub. To begin with, I wasn't certain you were the killer at that point. All I knew was that somebody with a second cannon was hidden nearby; and if I made a wrong move there might be some more blasting. Kay herself might get slugged. I wanted to protect her because I realized she was innocent. Then, later, I could start tracking the concealed gunsel."

"Oh," he summoned a sneer. "You realized Kay was innocent, eh? What did you have, a crystal ball or a cup of tea leaves?"

I peeled back my coat. "Something better than that," I grunted. "I'd heard two shots, so close together that the second one sounded almost like an echo of the first. Your wife's pill couldn't have creamed Squirrel-Puss because her aim was lousy."

"Really?"

"Yeah. She missed him clean, hit the communicating door *and nicked me on the shoulder.*" Then I gave him a hinge at the wound in the fleshy part of my flipper; the shallow gouge that had been aching like an ulcerated tooth for quite a while.

"My God . . .!" he whispered.

I SAID: "That's how I knew Kay wasn't guilty of murder. Somebody else had bumped the little guy; someone who savvied all about the setup in Room 607 of the Constantine, and who knew Kay was packing a rod. You matched those specifications. Most likely you had worked her up to the point of buying a roscoe to cool her supposed blackmailer; and you figured to back the play with your own bullet in case she missed."

He shuddered; seemed unable to say anything.

"The rest was routine," I finished. "I checked up on you by calling a gossip columnist; learned you were paying the apartment rent of a wren named Lucette Landon. That supplied the motive. You'd never been in love with Kay; you'd married her for her fortune. Now that you had it, a hunch hit me you might be planning to blow town with your sweetie. So I came here; put on an act to make you jealous when you arrived. It worked; threw you off your guard. Now you're washed up."

The brunette Landon frill butted in with a yowl of frustrated rage. "What about me? I never got anything out of the deal except my rent and a lot of promises! I didn't know the chiseling heel was going to k-kill anybody!"

"For which you can be thankful," I told her grimly. "A jane in your spot shouldn't complain."

She gave me the coquettish glimpse. "I'm not complaining . . . if you'll stick around, handsome."

"Not by a long shot," I backed off. "I've got other plans." And I washed my hands of the whole mess, left the details for Donaldson to clean up while I made knots to my own apartment stash.

Kay Vaughan was still there. I broke the news to her bluntly; told her the whole score. "So now you're in the clear, sweet stuff," I wound up the ugly story. "Your hubby did the dirty work and tried to pin it on you."

Two droplets of brine as big as mock oranges spilled out of her peepers, skidded down her wan cheeks. "To th-think Toby was the real blackmail-er . . ." she whispered. "Wh-why, the money I was pay-ing out was to buy back letters which he himself had written to some g-girl!"

"What?"

"Y-yes! It was his name I was trying to keep from scandal, not my own. . . ." All of a sudden she piped the gore on my shoulder. A tender expression came into her glims. "You —you're bleeding! I did th-that to you—!"

"Just a scratch," I shrugged.

"Scratch or no scratch, you've g-got to let me fix you up!"

So I let her fix me up. . . . She made a good nurse.

# FALL GUY FOR FORGERY

Hollywood's heftiest hawkshaw had faced cool feminine ferocity before, but never in so peculiar a shakedown racket as this one in which some louse was impersonating Dan to his great discredit and thereby incurring for the celebrated shamus the almost murderous savagery of two shapely cinematown sisters whose aim was to please—themselves!

T HE RUSSET-haired wren with the roscoe was sitting in a blue convertible coupe parked at the curb on Hollywood Boulevard, and minding her own business until I ankled abreast of her. Then she said casually: "Can you spare a moment, Mr. Turner?"

"Who, me?" I stopped in my tracks, pinned the admiring focus on her and wondered if maybe she was making a mistake. As far as I knew I'd never seen her before, although apparently she savvied my monicker well enough. "You mean me, tutz?"

She nodded. "I want to ask you something. That is, if you've got time to answer."

For a doll of her gorgeous specifications I would gladly have taken all the time there was, I reflected wolfishly—not knowing of course, that she was grasping a pearl-handled automatic in her dainty duke. The five-o'clock quitting whistle had just tootled and I had closed my office, drifted downstairs to the street with visions of driving home to my bachelor apartment for a few snifters of Vat 69 before showering and going out to a solitary supper, I had to pass this blue heap, though, in order to reach my own jalopy; at which juncture the jane with the ginger tresses gave me the come-hither eye.

When that happened I suddenly saw my plans al-

tering; figured I might have delishful she-male company with my evening repast. Had I suspected the chick was packing heat it would have been a different scenario entirely; I'd have helped myself to a prompt powder, scrammed in a cloud of peanut brittle. After all, when a guy has been around as long as I have he learns that quails toting firearms can be dangerous playmates; one untimely twitch of the trigger finger can make an angel of the toughest mug in shoe leather. Unfortunately you couldn't pipe her rod from where I was standing; and like a sap I barged close to her streamlined bucket, never guessing that I was sticking my neck out like a giraffe in a foxhole.

"You are Dan Turner, aren't you?" she added as I moved toward her.

"Yeah," I said.

"The private detective" she persisted.

I planted a brogan on the blue convertible's rudimentary runningboard and said: "So I've been led to believe by the telephone book. Now, then, I'm ready for that question you said you craved to ask me about. Shoot me the query, dearie."

"Shoot you—?" she sounded a trifle startled. Then she laughed. "Oh, yes, the query. It's a very simple one." She shifted her patent-leather handbag so that it no longer concealed the miniature cannon in the hand that rested on her lap. "Tell me what this is, Mr. Turner."

I tensed and yodeled: "Hey, what the hell! Point that gat the other way."

"Why?"

"Because it might go off, that's why."

She made a grim mouth. "That's esactly what'll happen—unless you do what I tell you to do. Now walk around quietly to the other side of my car. Get in. Drive."

"Hey, now wait—"

"And I warn you, if you try to run I'll send a bullet straight through your slimy heart."

AS a sample of melodramatic dialogue that sounded auspiciously like something out of a B picture from Poverty Row. But when I pinned the flabbergasted swivel on her I realized she was leveling. There was a deadly, resolute glitter in her greenish glims; her kisser was compressed to a thin crimson line of determination, emphasizing the threat she had just delivered. And yet, in spite of all this cool feminine ferocity, her map was prettier than a magazine cover. She had a complexion like cream poured on ripe peaches, there were three little freckles across her patrician smeller, and her wavy hair was a rich natural shade that had never got its tint from a henna rinse. On her face alone she could have been an Atlantic City beauty-contest winner without half trying.

She was strictly Miss America in the curves department, too. It takes a cookie with contours to wear the kind of sweater which currently embellished her—to say nothing of her stems stretched up under the instrument panel, shapely and tapered in leg makeup that did an excellent job of imitating nylons. Even her pert white sports skirt was nice scenery, although I couldn't give it my complete attention as long as she was aiming her fowling-piece at me. That spoiled the picture.

For an instant I debated the wisdom of reaching over her door, making a wild grab for the roscoe. Then I decided not to; the odds were against me. She could plug me while I was still reaching; it was too long a chance. So I made the best of the bad deal; I shrugged and walked around to the far side of her chariot, slid my tonnage under the wheel.

"Sensible you," she commented tartly.

I said: "Yeah, but why all this gangster routine? Shucks, hon, you could have got the same results with a kind smile instead of that Flit gun you're brandishing. I'm a soft touch for redheads; always have been."

"Blondes too?" her voice was taut.

"Well, yeah," I admitted. "I guess you might say I'm a fool for blondes, depending on the blondes."

"You're a fool, period. And you're a heel. Now shut up. Get going. Drive."

I kicked the starter, chose a gear, eased out the clutch with great care; I didn't want a jerky start to touch off any fireworks. We rolled forward into the Boulevard traffic stream and I tabbed more than one misguided bozo dishing me the envious gander for my elegant equipage and my toothsome companion. To look at me nobody would have guessed

there was a heater nudging me in the short ribs and sputtering on a clipped fuse.

After a few blocks went by I said: "Where are we headed, sweet stuff?"

"Just keep going west."

"Oh. Secret destination, eh?"

"Not at all. Drive straight ahead until you come to a street marked Nichols Canyon Road. Then turn right."

"And if I should beef to the first traffic cop we

pass?"

"Try it," she dared me, and I heard a click as she unlatched the automatic's safety mechanism.

"You really mean you'd drill me?"

"Like a mad dog," she said. There was another sample of that B-picture dialogue. The way she spoke it, though, made it sound too sincere for comfort.

I hunched my shoulders, settled down to my driving. As far as I was concerned the luscious lassie alongside me was loco; but the knowledge brought me very little peace of mind. A dippy dame could shoot me just as defunct as a sane one—only sooner and for less reason.

THAT was what pestered me. I'd never done anything to merit a bullet prescription from the ginger-haired jessie; in fact, I had never even met her before. The oftener I copped a sidewise swivel at her stern pan the more positive I was that she and I were total strangers. Then why should she be putting the snatch on me and threatening to blast me if I squawked? It simply didn't add up to make sense.

Presently we came to Nichols Canyon and I swung into it under the lengthening shadows of a long row of pepper trees that thickened the gathering dusk. The frill with the russet coiffure said: "Sixth house on your left."

"Okay."

"Steer across that little bridge over the drainage ditch and stop in the driveway."

I obeyed orders; fastened the parking anchors. "Now what?" I inquired meekly.

"We go inside."

Hope slithered into my nooks and crannies. "All right. Lead the way, lady."

"Wouldn't you just love that!" she jeered. "Oh, no. You first. You're not jumping me from behind, wise guy." She jammed the spout of her weapon ferninst one of my favorite kidneys, prodded me to the porch of a rambling igloo that had seen better days. It was still a fairly sumptuous stash, dripping wistaria and honeysuckle vines that filled the air with fragrance; but the woodwork under the vines needed fresh paint and the formal garden had been allowed to go to seed, indicating a lack of dough for upkeep. Four or five centuries, spent judiciously, would have done wonders for the joint. On the other hand, maybe that would have meant slapping a mortgage on the blue convertible.

I was curious.

The front door of the stash was ajar. I was shoved over the threshold into a cozy living-room that seemed exclusively feminine; the window drapes were frilly chintz, the furniture gay with slip covers of the same bright material and the ashtrays loaded with lipstick-stained cigarette butts. No cigars, though. And all the scattered magazines were the romantic kind—*Amour, Magic Love, Leading Love* and the like, with a few fashion journals thrown in for good measure. But I didn't see any copies of *Esquire*.

"No male inhabitants, eh, babe?" I turned to the redhead.

"What gives you that idea?"

"I'm a detective."

"Yes, so you are. Also a louse."

I gave her a resigned smile. "Well, that seems to take care of the small talk. What comes next?"

"This," she rasped, and clouted me lustily on the noggin with the barrel of her gat.

## CHAPTER II
*Odd Retainer*

THE SWAT didn't drop me; but it had plenty of steam behind it, enough to scramble my grey matter for a few seconds. While I was still staggering off-balance the cookie tripped me sprawling. Her jiu-jitsu routine caught me with my guard at half mast and I fell on my profile, dented the rug with my trumpet. Temporarily I heard nothing but bells and birdies; then I became conscious of drapery cords being looped and tightened around my wrists and ankles. By the time the fog drifted out of my anguished peepers I was trussed like a calf at branding season.

I was also as sore as a picked blister. "Now see

here, dammit!" I caterwauled indignantly. "This is a free country. I'm a citizen and a taxpayer. You can't do this to me!"

"You don't say," she murmured, and barged out of the living-room. She came back a moment later with a delectable little blonde muffin in tow: a doll who looked enough like her to be her sister. At a guess, I estimated this yellow-haired quail to be maybe two or three years younger than the one with the ginger tresses, but she was every bit as pretty. Her plump figure was very soothing to the optics, particularly since she was garnished in a gossamer negligee of pale green chiffon—a vision doubly enchanting from my angle where I was stretched out on the floor.

Her piquant countenance, however, was a mask of misery and woe. Droplets of brine brimmed in her azure glims and tremulous grief twisted her kisser.

The redhead gave her a nudge. "There he is, Barbara. Go on—give him what he deserves. Kick the filthy creep."

"Hey, ix-nay!" I yeeped. "No fair! You don't boot a guy when he's down. It's against the rules."

Ignoring me, my russet-haired hostess again said to the curvaceous blonde cutie: "Kick him, Barbara. Hard."

"But . . . but Sis!" the younger wren wailed. "He isn't . . . I mean I c-can't—"

"Why can't you? Go ahead, stomp on his face."

"No! That's n-not the m-man!"

"Not the man? Don't be silly. This is Dan Turner. He told me so himself." She peered down at me spitefully. "Didn't you?"

I said: "Yeah, much to my regret."

"But he isn't the Dan Turner w-who . . . who gypped me!" All of a sudden the woeful one pivoted, pelted hellity-blip from the room with her gossamer green negligee trailing cloudily behind her. As she vanished you could hear her muffled sobs receding toward the back of the tepee.

THIS left me alone with the redhead of the sweater and white sports skirt. I squirmed against my fetters, glued the irate gander on her and gave vent to an infuriated bellow. "So I'm not the Dan Turner that gypped her!" I grated. "If that remark makes any sense I'm a demented Senegambian."

"Oh, please, Mr. Turner—"

"Maybe it's your idea of a rib," I sneered. "If so, I fail to appreciate the joke. Untie me and I'll slap the everlasting bejaspers out of you."

She fluttered toward me, leaned down, plucked at the knots in jittery haste. "I . . . I don't know what to say, Mr. Turner. It's all such a fantastic mistake!"

"Yeah," I said the instant I was loose. Then I surged upright and fastened the grab on her, shook her until her grinders clattered like dice in a fist. "Yeah, it's all a fantastic mistake. Only that's not enough explanation."

She didn't fight me, didn't struggle to free herself from my clutches. "I g-guess you've got a right to ask questions," her tone was doleful and her glims contrite. They should have been.

"Damned right I have. Now scream the scenario." I released her, got a strangle hold on my temper and set fire to a gasper just to give my fingers something to do. "Start talking."

"Well, I . . . I . . . that is—"

"Let's have your name first."

"I . . . I'm Sally Elliott. I'm a stock actress at Metrovox; I do bit parts."

"Contract?"

She nodded. "Unless they d-drop my option next month. And the g-girl who was just in here is my k-kid sister Barbara."

"So I gathered. Is she in the galloping snapshots-too?" I glowered at her.

"N-no. She'd like to be, of course; who wouldn't? But she never has been able to land a movie job. Why do you ask?"

"I thought I'd seen her somewhere before, is all. Skip it. Go ahead and tell me why you yearned to load me with lumps."

She got pink around the fringes. "Well, some-thing p-pretty ugly happened to Barbara this after-noon. She met a man in a cocktail bar."

"Happens all the time."

"Yes, but this man said he was Dan Turner, the famous private detective—"

My knuckles commenced to get itchy. "You mean he was impersonating me?"

"It looks that w-way, now. Anyway, he told Bar-bara he had lots of influence and could get her into a big feature production. If I had been there to warn her it would have been different; but she believed him, poor kid."

"And then what?" I said.

"They had some drinks. Barbara isn't a good drinker. She can't hold it too well. She got a little dizzy, and . . . and—"

"Don't tell me he invited her to see his etchings?"

"Something like that. Not quite. He said his apartment was just a couple of blocks away and offered to take her there to sober her up. Besides, he said he wanted to talk to her some more about this job in pictures."

I said sourly: "I can guess the rest. She went with him; passed out when she got to his drop. Then the dirty rat—"

"Oh, no, Mr. Turner, it wasn't that way at all. Quite the contrary. He gave her black coffee and a bromo; treated her like any gentleman treats a lady."

"Now I've heard everything," I said. "The guy was nuts, eh?"

"No, he was a thief."

I stared at her. "Come again?"

"He said it would take a little bribing to get her a fat role in this movie he'd mentioned. He asked her how much cash she had and she told him about fifty dollars. That wasn't enough. He took it but he wanted more, a lot more. He persuaded her to write him a check for three hundred—which was just about all Barbara and I had in our joint bank account. Not only that, but she gave him an emerald brooch and a little diamond ring she was wearing; jewelry mother left her when she died. Not worth very much, perhaps, but valuable to us. Keepsakes, you know."

"And?"

She sighed. "That's about all. Maybe he couldn't

have pawned the ring and brooch for more than a hundred and fifty, all told; but add that to the fifty dollars cash she gave him, and the check for three hundred—that's five hundred dollars. He cashed the check, too; I know that much. I phoned the bank and asked them the moment Barbara told me what she'd done."

"When *did* she tell you?"

"As soon as she came home, around three-thirty. I realized as soon as I heard about it that she'd been taken in by a sharper, a cheap chiseling crooked private dick."

I said: "Hey, hold it. Lay off that crooked-private-dick talk. She just admitted I'm not the guy that clipped her."

"Yes, I know. But I thought you were the man. We even had the signature on a receipt he gave her."

"Receipt?" I choked. "He had the gall to do that?"

SHE nodded, went and got her purse. opened it, dug forth a slip of paper and handed it to me. Sure enough, it had my name signed at the bottom; but the forgery didn't even resemble my scrawl. It was as if somebody had written the words "Dan Turner" without ever having seen an original.

"Now you know why I waylaid you and brought you here," the red-haired Sally Elliot faltered forlornly. "I wanted Barbara to get even with you for what you'd d-done. I even thought maybe we could force you to give back some of the money whatever you hadn't spent in the meantime. Only you're the wrong m-man."

"Yeah," I said. "That's understandable."

"You .. you aren't sore? You'll f-forgive me?"

"Skip it," I told her airily. "The main thing is to locate this loogan before he pulls any more of his shenanigans."

"Locate him? You . . . you mean you want to hunt for him and have a showdown?"

"But definitely," I said. "Now call Barbara back so I can ask her if she remembers the address of the apartment where the skunk took her. And what he looked like. No use flying blind when she's got the information."

The blonde muffin must have been eavesdropping in the adjoining room, because she joined us without waiting for an invitation. "I can tell you the place," she said tonelessly. "It was a shabby walkup over on Rampart!' She mentioned the location and the number of the flat: 209, second floor rear.

I said: "Swell. Now describe him."

"He was tall, thin, sallow. He had sandy hair," she answered. "And he wore a grey serge suit. Not very well pressed, either. It looked kind of seedy!'

I thanked her, turned to her ginger-topped older sister. "How about driving me back downtown to my jalopy, hon?"

She agreed; seemed eager to make amends for the way she'd pushed me around. We hauled bunions out to her spiffy blue convertible and got going; left the younger wren moping in the wigwam.

It was dark when we drew up alongside my vee-eight coupe back on Hollywood Boulevard a little later. The Elliot frail twisted around, faced me, dished me a timorous smile. "Y-you have forgiven me for the things I did to you, haven't you, Mr. Turner?"

"Sure. Now scram."

She hesitated before she clashed her gears. "Wh-what about the fee?" she asked me. "I c-can't expect you to start looking for that confidence man without being p-paid."

"Aw, forget it," I told her. "This is on the house. When some sharp orange starts forging my name on phony receipts and impersonating me for ulterior purposes it's my job to nail him. Besides, if he took your sister and you to the cleaners you haven't got a retainer to pay me."

She admitted: "No," and gave me an inscrutable,

enigmatic smile. Then she drove off; left me to wonder if . . . .

## CHAPTER III
### *Whim of a Female?*

I SCRAMBLED into my chariot, rammed it toward Rampart Street under forced draft. Presently I gained my destination; barged into a two-story rookery that stank of stale cooking and last night's gin. I catfooted upstairs; ducked into an alcove as I spotted a guy coming down the hallway in my direction. I couldn't be sure, but it struck me he had just emerged from Apartment 209—which was the flat I wanted.

He passed the alcove without noticing me, but I glommed a perfect swivel at his puss as he went by. He was a chunky, swarthy character, nothing at all like the description the blonde Barbara Elliot had given me of the guy who'd rooked her; so I knew he wasn't the guilty ginzo. Somehow, though, this beefy party now passing me seemed familiar, as if I'd seen him before—and, moreover, recently.

I prodded my mental cogwheels, tried to tab him. Abruptly the gears meshed, clicked out the answer. He was Flash Raudello—an unsavory jackleg with a rotten rep in the cinema colony. Baudello ran what purported to be a legitimate studio-talent agency out on the Sunset Strip; but in reality he specialized in supplying honkytonk entertainment for stag smokers: kootchie dancers, strippers, off-color singers, slot machines and floating roulette layouts, crap games, the sort of thing you usually find at a professionally produced stag party. I myself had been to one of his clambakes a week or so before, which was where I'd encountered him directing the activities.

Oddly enough, the guy had never been knocked over by the vice squad for his traffic in the brand of shows frowned upon by Purity Leaguers. Maybe this was because he was smart enough to keep covered. At least he'd been clever enough to stay out of the bastille, although everybody in Hollywood knew he was as crooked as a bag of pretzels. Right now, though, he looked excited, jittery. He was breathing hard, his peepers bulged like two spoiled oysters and his complexion was a sickly greenish grey as he scurried down the staircase. You couldn't tell whether he was scared or just plain infuriated; possibly it was a mixture of both.

I waited until I figured he was out of sight; then I ankled from my hiding place. Right away I saw I'd made my move too soon; Baudello was still at the bottom of the steps, shoving something into his topcoat pocket. I ducked again; wondered if he had lamped me.

Presently I heard him go out of the building. That relieved my mind; I didn't want anybody to witness what I intended to do to the unknown slob who had masqueraded under my moniker. I let ten seconds go by, then made for the door marked 209 and thumped it with my knuckles.

Nobody answered.

I rapped again. Still it was no dice. On a hunch I tried the knob and it turned in my grasp; the latch was unfastened. I shoved the portal inward; tiptoed cautiously over the threshold. The room was darker than the inside of an ink bottle, but I thought I sensed motion somewhere before me—faint, furtive, the merest whisper of sound.

Some sixth sense warned me of danger. I was silhouetted in the open doorway with a dim corridor light at my back; this made me a perfect clay pigeon if anybody in the room craved to indulge in target practice. And that sound I had heard seemed subtly metallic, like the muffled cocking of a roscoe's hammer across the room. I wasn't reassured.

You need quick reflexes in the snooping racket and mine were functioning at full velocity. I flung myself forward, dived desperately and scraped my mush on the carpet just as the surrounding velvet blackness was stabbed wide open by a spurt of golden flame. A flat, barking *ka-chee!* sneezed at the spot I'd been occupying an instant ago, and the air was suddenly acrid with the fumes of burned gunpowder.

All in one movement I rolled sidewise, whipped my own roscoe from the shoulder holster where I always carry it for emergencies; triggered a pair of pills toward where that flame-flash had blazed. I fired so fast that my cannon's twin reports blended together, sounded almost like one single thunderous roar. Then I rolled again, waiting to see what would happen next.

Silence settled, thick as curds. Presently I risked rising on all fours. I pulled my pencil flash, started to thumb a beam out of it—

*Pow!* Something crashed down on the back of my cranium as if the roof had caved in. Neon lights pinwheeled in my agonized peepers and gongs clanged in my ears. I was the guy for whom those bells tolled. I toppled, folded like an accordion and took a nice long trip to slumberland.

WHEN I snapped out of my coma the stash was lighted brighter than a Christmas tree and crawling with coppers. Evidently some of the neighbors had put in a bleat to headquarters after hearing the pistol picnic, and now the bulls were on hand in full panoply—including my friend Dave Donaldson of the homicide squad.

Dave was hunkering his hulk alongside me, splatting me across the chops with his beefy palm. He kept saying: "Wake up, wise guy. Wake up and spill or I'll kick the damnation French pastry out of you. Come on, the possum act isn't fooling me."

I stirred feebly, moaned, glued the groggy gander

on him. "Go away."

"Yeah? I said quit playing possum!"

"Possum my adenoids," I whinnied. "Take your halitosis out of here. I'm a sick man."

He snarled: "You'll be a hell of a lot sicker before I'm done with you, Hawkshaw. Don't you know any better than to croak a policeman?"

"Hah?" I sat on my haunches, blinked at him.

"Well, anyhow, a former policeman," he amended. "Any way you look at it, it's murder."

His words brought me staggering to a perpendicular stance in a hell of a yank. The blur drifted

out of my grey matter and the knot on the rear of my conk quit throbbing; or anyhow I stopped paying attention to it. I was too busy grabbing a slant at the far side of the room and realizing the triple-distilled dimensions of the jackpot I was in.

There was an easy chair against the wall, with a skinny bozo slumped in its shabbily upholstered depths—a yuck with sandy hair, a sallow map and glassy, wide-open glimmers. He was wearing an unpressed grey serge suit and he had twin holes in the front of his shirt, spang through the bellows. When I mentally measured the distance and the angle between the chair and the apartment's doorway I knew those were my slugs cluttering up the guy's clockworks. I had drilled him plumb center with my two shots, and now he was deader than a dish of fried tripe.

I blinked at Donaldson. "You say he was a cop?"

"Yeah. Ex-cop. Used to work on the vice detail, name of Eberfeldt. Percival Eberfeldt." Dave lifted a lip. "As if you didn't know."

"I never saw him before," I announced earnestly. "I've heard of him, though. They used to call him Perce for short, only they spelled it Purse because he was always dipping into somebody's—I mean he took graft. The way I got it. Right?"

Dave made a grim mouth. "Right on the button, so don't claim you didn't know him."

"I didn't know him," I repeated. "Only by hearsay."

"Then why'd you cool him down?"

I said: "Self-defense."

"Oh, come now."

"It's true!" I grated. "He fired at me first."

"Don't fed me that sheep-dip." Dave's broad mush darkened. "The neighbors heard only two shots, and there's two bullets in the guy—which accounts for both reports. If he had blasted at you it would have made a third explosion, and there wasn't any third explosion."

"That's because mine were spaced so close together that they sounded practically like one," I said. "I'm fast on the trigger; you know that. You've shot with me on the target range."

"For the last time, though," he said, scowling. "You'll do no more shooting from here on out. You're headed for the gas house unless you can think up a more plausible story."

I matched his scowl with one of my own. "I'm standing pat on the truth—the truth being what I just told you."

"That he fired at you first?"

"Yeah."

"It won't work, gumshoe. While you were snoozing we frisked this room from stem to gudgeon; also the hallway outside the door. And we didn't find any slugs in the walls."

"So what?" I said.

"So if Eberfeldt had shot at you before you blasted him, we'd have found a chunk of lead somewhere. But we didn't. Therefore he didn't fire at you."

I said: "Nuts. You probably didn't search hard enough."

"The hell we didn't. In fact, we even carried it a step further. We made a quick paraffin test of Eberfeldt's hands."

"And?"

"Negative," Dave said. "Proving he hadn't triggered a rod."

THIS information left me a trifle sandbagged. Finally I recovered some of my poise. "He did trigger it. He must have. Damn it, I tell you he took a potshot at me and I fired at the flash. Then I got bludgeoned senseless; didn't wake up until now."

Dave treated me to a supercilious leer. "You expect me to believe you, shoved two lumps into the guy's ticker and then he got up, maced you unconscious and went back to his chair before he kicked the bucket? Don't be foolish, gumshoe. That's ridiculous and you damned well know it."

"Oh, I suppose I festooned this bump on my own scalp, eh?" I challenged him.

"You might have. It's been done. How the hell do I know what goes on in that dizzy brain of yours?" Then he added: "How do I know what brought you here in the first place?"

"I can explain that in very few words," I said. "This Percival Eberfeldt character is a perfect fit to the description I was given of a party who impersonated me, clipped a dame for five Cs and forged my name to a receipt."

"You're kidding!" He looked startled.

"In a pig's knuckle I'm kidding." And I fed him the whole plot-line, beginning with my original encounter with the red-haired Sally Elliot and carrying it on through the events that had happened to her younger sister, Barbara. I omitted no details; it was no time to hold back information. Not from him.

When I got through sounding off at the yapper, Dave muttered: "Hm-m-m-. So you think Eberfeldt was the one who gypped this Barbara Elliot, do you?"

"Well, he's thin. He's got sandy hair and a sallow complexion. And he's wearing a seedy grey serge suit. Moreover, this is the apartment where he brought her and put the bite on her for dough, a check and some jewelry. You figure it up."

He scratched his chin stubble, noisily. "You know, I've had a suspicion Eberfeldt was shady. A vice-squad detective gets plenty of chance to go crooked if he's inclined that way, and he was. That's why he got fired off the force."

"Everybody knows that."

"Yeah, but I mean after he turned in his badge.

For a while he tried to get a private license but the board turned him down; his record was against him. Still, he seemed to get by. He never had a pocketful, but he was always good for his rent and meals. Played the horses now and then, too. So where was he getting his moolah?"

I said: "The confidence racket, obviously."

He meditated for a few moments and presently muttered:

"I think you're right, Sherlock. Which makes me believe maybe there's a way out of this mess for you."

"How so?"

Dave said:

"If we can expose him as a forger and a gyp artist it'll demonstrate that you had a legitimate reason for coming here to his apartment."

"Make it plainer," I said.

He spread his mitts, palm up. "You were checking on him for a deal he had pulled—this bite he put on Barbara Elliot. We'll say he was scared you were going to turn him in to the law, so he hit you with a blunt instrument and tried to smash your skull. That's when you shot him, killed him. No jury is going to convict you for that. As a mutter of fact bet you won't even be indicted to stand trial."

"But that wasn't the way it happened," I argued. "I didn't get bopped until after I plugged him."

"Keep that part under your hat," Dave grunted.

"That only complicates it, and why borrow trouble? Don't be a chump. I'm trying to pull you out of the grease, fireball."

"But—"

"Shut up. I'll send one of my men out to pick up those Elliot girls and bring them here. If they back up your yarn I'll probably turn you loose on your own recognizance; won't even book you. Satisfied?"

I said: "Sure, but suppose the janes won't want to come here? What then?"

"You worry too much. I'll have them here by the time the medical examiner shows up to take a look at Eberfeldt's corpse." Whereupon he issued the necessary instructions to a flatfoot standing nearby. The flatfoot saluted, executed a smart right-about-face, stumbled, almost fell on his dewlaps, and departed, muttering something about being subject to spells of vertigo.

SPEAKING of vertigo, my own noggin had commenced to throb again; so I started prowling the premises in search of a snort of pain killer. My optimism was unfounded; there wasn't a drop of whisky in the joint. I did run into something else, though. It was in a kitchenette cupboard behind a stack of canned tomatoes: a bank passbook, with Percival Eberfeldt's name on the front inside page. The book recorded a long string of deposits, but they weren't on regular dates as they would have been if they represented salary checks. Beyond that, the amounts were inconsistent; one week they'd be high, another week low. Some weeks there wouldn't be any deposits at all; other times several within a few days. If you could judge by the inked figures, Eberfeldt's income had been gathered from a large number of sources, and not on any stipulated collection dates.

I torched a coffin nail, tried to find logic in what the bank book told me. Gyppery had evidently paid the former vice-squad cop a living wage; but some of the deposits looked too big to be the fruits of small-time con games. There were some shakedown payoffs, too, I decided. Maybe blackmail as well. A guy of Eberfeldt's caliber would probably try his fist at anything crooked—as long as it wasn't too dangerous.

While I was thinking about it, Donaldson called to me from the living-room. "Hey, Hawkshaw, the Elliot girls are here."

That was what I'd been waiting for. I hotfooted from the kitchenette, piped the luscious sisters standing by the front doorway. Sally, the one with the russet coiffure, was still garbed in that tight sweater and pert white skirt. Barbara, however, didn't look quite so gorgeous now that she had traded her filmy green negligee for a frock of garish red satin that clung to her curves like lacquer. The outfit was too blatant; besides which, her makeup was heavier than necessary. It gave her a tough, almost a skidrow, appearance.

Not that it mattered. I wasn't judging a beauty show; what I wanted was corroboration. I said: "Hi, girls. Sorry to be a nuisance, but I need you both to get me out from behind a very black eight ball."

Sally patted her ginger locks, gave me the frosty focus. "Do you mind explaining what you mean, please? I'm afraid there's a mistake somewhere. I don't know you."

"Don't know me?" I strangled. "Why, I—"

She turned to Donaldson. "Who is that man and what does he want?"

"Now just a minute!" I yelped, barging toward her in a towering tizzy. "You know who I am. I'm Dan Turner. Don't tell me you've forgotten so soon, Kitten!"

"You must be out of your mind," she snapped. "I've never seen you before in my life."

## CHAPTER IV
### Complications Are Cruel

FOR a thunderstruck instant my knees turned to boiled noodles and I felt my map getting fiery red. Then I surged close to her, grabbed her. "What the hell are you trying to pull on me?" I roared. "Now cut it out!"

"You let Sally alone!" the blonde Barbara

screeched like a banshee and flurried at me, clawing. "Let go of her before I scratch your dirty eyes out!"

I fended her off. "Calm down! Look, let's not play games. A guy has just been plugged to his ancestors and I'm under the gun for it. You two janes have got to explain to these cops that I've been working for you."

"Working for us?" Sally's peepers narrowed as she pulled free of my clutch and sided with her blonde younger sister. "That's utterly crazy."

I got a throttle hold on my mounting temper. "Let's start all over," I said. "I realize neither one of you wants to get mixed up in a homicide beef. I know you don't want the newspapers printing the story because you'd sooner avoid unfavorable publicity—you, Sally, especially, on account of your stock-actress contract with Metrovox Pix. You've got an option coming up next month, and you don't want them to drop it. But—"

"Why should my sister be afraid of newspaper publicity?" Barbara horned in. "Murder or no murder, she's got nothing to do with it and neither have I."

I said: "Quit clowning, babe. String with me and maybe we can keep it out of the headlines."

"Keep what out of the headlines?"

"How Eberfeldt got you plastered and brought you here to his apartment and chewed you for five hundred hermans on a phony promise to get you a movie job," I said.

At this, Sally tossed her ginger mane. "Now I'm sure you must be insane. Barbara never paid anybody five hundred dollars to get a movie job. She doesn't want a movie job. She's too busy keeping house for me." She glared at me.

"Do you mean to stand there with your teeth in your mouth and claim—"

"I haven't the foggiest idea what you're talking about."

I whirled to Donaldson. "Could you possibly look the other way while I slap some truth out of these frails, pal?"

"Sorry." He shook his head. "No more rough stuff, Philo. Your jig is up."

"Meaning exactly what?"

"Meaning you're under arrest for killing Purse Eberfeldt, and let's have no more lip about it. Come on, I'm taking you downtown to the gow."

FROM the other side of the room a new voice suddenly busted into the dialogue. It belonged to the medical examiner, who'd arrived a little while before, and who had been busily inspecting the defunct guy's remnants in the overstuffed chair. Now he said: "Wait just a minute, Lieutenant Donaldson."

"Wait for what?" Dave glared at him truculently.

"I'm afraid you can't place Mr. Turner in custody for murder—at least not on the basis of his bullets in the corpse."

"Wh-wha-what was that you said?"

"I said you can't arrest Turner for murdering this man. Or at least you can't arrest him for shooting him."

Dave's cheeks got purple. "Lay off that double-talk!" he rasped. "Speak English."

"What does it sound like, Sanskrit?" the medico bridled. "Look. Once and for all I'm telling you Turner didn't shoot Eberfeldt to death."

"You're nuts! He even admits he shot him."

"But not to death," the doctor said coolly. "I mean his slugs were not the cause of death. To make it plainer, Eberfeldt was already dead when Turner shot him. Now do I make myself clear or do I have to draw you a diagram?"

Dave lurched drunkenly and started to chew a fingernail, only he made a mistake and gnawed the finger instead. "Ouch!" he yelped indignantly, glaring at himself in a mirror over the imitation fireplace mantel. Then: "Well, if Eberfeldt was already dead when Turner shot him, then what the hell killed him? Eberfeldt, I mean."

"He was struck over the head. His skull was crushed. Come see for yourself if you want to."

Dave tottered toward the chair, copped a bleary swivel. "Holy jumping jeep, you're right!"

"Natch." The medico preened himself. "I'm always right." He absently wiped a red-stained scalpel on Eberfeldt's necktie. Eberfeldt, being deceased, didn't seem to mind.

Dave whirled like a dervish with the hotfoot; grabbed hold of my lapels. "So okay, bright eyes. You brained the guy before you plugged him through the chest. That explains it. That's how you got that lump on your own conk. You had a hell of a brawl with Eberfeldt and he managed to mace you before you finally swatted him dead. Then you blasted a couple of pills in him in a crazy effort to give yourself an out. Now come clean and do it fast. What was your motive?"

"Aw, lay off," I said wearily. "I've already admitted I shot him, sure; but if he was defunct when I did it, you can't hang a homicide rap on me. Boring holes in a cadaver isn't a capital offense in California."

"Stew that. I'm charging you with cooling him by hitting him with a blackjack or something."

"That's where you're haywire, you dope. Somebody else got to him ahead of me, and bashed in his steeple before I had a chance to put the arm on him for forging my name on a gyp receipt. He must have been a stiff when I got here."

"Still insisting on that forgery story, hah?"

"Yeah. And I could prove it to the hilt if these Elliot cookies weren't so damned scared of being smeared with a publicity scandal."

The red-haired Sally made a casual gesture of

patting back a yawn. "Barbara and I don't know anything about it."

"See, fireball?" Dave glowered. "Your forged-receipt scenario falls just as flat as your claim that Eberfeldt triggered a shot at you before you went for your own rod. You're lying like a taxi meter."

I screeched: "But he did fire first! Almost got me, too."

"Yeah? How could he, if he was dead when you walked in?"

THE logic of that speech stopped me cold; and then, suddenly, I commenced remembering various details that arranged themselves in a swiftly unfolded pattern. When the pattern was completed, I had the riddle's answer. "Flash Baudello!" I said.

Dave slitted his optics. "What about Flash Baudello? Who is he and what difference does it make who he is?"

"He's a big beefy skunk, a talent agent," I said. "He was here tonight."

"Oh, so?"

"Yeah. I tabbed him as he barged out of this very flat—and I've got a hunch he may be a key to the kill."

"Dream on," Dave said sarcastically. But I could tell he was interested in spite of that. "Granting there is a guy named Flash Baudello and he's a talent agent and he was here tonight, how is he a key to the

218

kill?"

I said: "Maybe he was paying protection dough to Eberfeldt to keep the vice squad off his neck. Baudello puts on stag shows. I mean the kind of stag shows that get raided."

"You're overlooking something," Dave sneered. "Eberfeldt was no longer a member of the vice detail; he'd been fired. Why would anybody pay him protection, then? He didn't drag any weight. You don't buy influence from a guy who hasn't any."

"Well, then, maybe it was shakedown money," I persisted. "We know Eberfeldt had been a grafter when he was on the force. Very likely he continued his grafting after he got canned. All he had to do was use the knowledge he'd picked up as a cop. Say he knew Baudello dealt in shady entertainment. So he goes to Baudello and demands a hush payoff, otherwise threatening to send an anonymous tip to the bulls which would result in Baudello getting in Dutch with the authorities for conducting illegal gambling games, booking strippers and kootch dancers and so forth. Baudello realizes Eberfeldt has got the goods on him, and, to avoid trouble, stands for a shakedown. A whole series of shakedowns. He keeps making a regular contribution to Eberfeldt, first because he can afford it and second because Eberfeldt's got him in a hole. Moreover, these blackmail touches aren't too severe at first. Eberfeldt's entries in his bank book prove he never collected any large sums from anybody; it was just a small but steady drain."

"Well?"

"So assume tonight was another payoff night, and Baudello arrives here to hand over his usual dab of sugar. Then suppose our pal Eberfeldt suddenly boosts the ante; makes a bigger demand than Baudello is accustomed to giving him. Baudello balks. They argue. The argument becomes a fracas. Baudelllo finally picks up something and bunts Eberfeldt on the crumpet, thereby rendering him into a corpse."

DAVE licked his lips as if he liked the taste of what I was saying. "Go on, keep it up."

"Sure. So now Eberfeldt is deceased. Baudello props the body in that chair and cops himself a scram. All right; I arrive just as Baudello is leaving. I can see he's upset, excited, maybe even scared—although naturally I can't guess why. Meantime I've got my own reasons for not wanting him to notice me, so I hide in an alcove at the head of the stairway. The trouble is, I come out of that alcove a bit too soon; and it's entirely possible that Baudello does spot me from the downstairs lobby. I'm not certain of this, but it begins to look—"

"Make your point," Dave said.

"Okay. So maybe Baudello ducks around to the side alley alongside the building. He climbs up the fire escape and gets back into this flat through that open window over there. Let's assume he crouches behind the chair containing Eberfeldt's cadaver, waiting for me to enter. I do. He fires a shot at me, reaching his gun hand around the chair until it's directly in front of the corpse's chest. He does this because he figures I'll return the fire, aiming at the flash of his roscoe. Which is exactly what I do, thereby pouring two slugs into Eberfeldt's dead lungs."

"A frame, hunh?"

"Sure. Baudello, having cracked Eberfeldt's skull open, has now baited me into shooting the murdered guy. The rest is simple. All Baudello has to do is blackjack me the way he did Eberfeldt—that is, hard enough to kill me. Then he can lam, leaving a pair of defunct parties in the room. Eberfeldt can't squeal, I can't squeal; it looks as if maybe we bumped each other off in a brawl. And that puts Baudello in the clear. However, there's an unexpected snag. Baudello doesn't bash me quite hard enough. I'm senseless but I'm not dead—thanks to my castiron scalp," I added fervently, rubbing the sore place.

Donaldson grew thoughtful, which gave him a pained expression. Then he said: "Nope."

"What do you mean, nope?"

"It's too glib, Philo. I don't believe a word of it."

"Well, for the love . . ."

"In fact, I don't even believe this Baudello guy was here at all. I'm not even sure there is anybody named Baudello. What have I got except your un-supported word, you being the liar you are? Nope, I'm not buying it."

"You've got to!" I bellowed. "I'm leveling. There is a Flash Baudello; you can check that easily enough. And he was here this evening."

"How can I check that part of it?"

I said sourly: "You can't. You just have to believe me."

"But I don't."

"Okay, be stubborn," I growled, "If you don't like the theory I just gave you, I'll give you an alternate."

"Could you make it short?"

"Yeah. It's possible Baudello came here to make a shakedown payoff and found Eberfeldt already croaked by some unknown character, Lamping the corpse, Baudello maybe got scared and scrammed."

"What unknown character?"

"That's your job to find out." I sulked. Then I relented, for a definite purpose. "Maybe Baudello even tabbed the murderer lurking here in the flat and beat it for fear of getting a dose of the same."

"What makes you think so?"

"I don't know; I'm just guessing now. You could find out, however."

"How?"

"By asking him," I said.

Dave mulled this over. "Not a bad idea. I'll put out a bleat for this alleged Baudello guy right now. Meantime, stick out your fins. I want to try these bracelets on you for size."

I stiffened. "What for?"

"You're not out of the woods yet," he said. "Until I get some better breaks I'm holding you on suspicion. Come on, tall, sharp and battered. Let's have your hands."

I said: "Okay. I'll give you the right one first."

Making a regretful fist, I tagged him on the lug and knocked him as cold as an Eskimo's tonsils.

## CHAPTER V
*Two-legged Poison*

IT WAS a scurvy trick to play on a pal, but I craved freedom in copious quantities. I knew damned well I couldn't do myself any good while languishing in the jug; and from where I stood, the future looked lousy unless I could start unraveling some knots. I'd already got some of the loose ends located, but there was still a big job ahead of me. So I dished Donaldson this haymaker, dumped him on his duff, leaped his quivering tonnage and made a wild dash for the door.

I gained it before any of Dave's astounded minions could snap out of their bewilderment; I rushed past Sally and Barbara Elliot so fast they didn't even have time to scream. I got to the stairway while everybody was still in a state of suspended animation; went pounding downward with my hip pockets dipping tacks. Twenty brief seconds subsequently I skyrocketed to the street, blammed into my jalopy, kicked it into forward motion and tore a gaping gash in the innocent night.

Flash Baudello was the bozo I craved to interview, and indeed soon—or my schedule would be fractured to hellangone. The trouble was, I didn't know where the chunky skunk hung out; and when I consulted a drugstore's city directory a little later, he wasn't in it. The census takers must have missed him; maybe they'd forgotten to look under all the rocks.

Next I tried telephoning his office on the Sunset Strip, the agency layout he used for a front to cover his less-legal business ventures. Nobody answered my jingle, though, and when I hung up I got my nickel back. I'd scarcely expected anyone to be there after office hours, anyhow.

Just the same, this put me over a barrel. Baudello's home phone was an unlisted connection, a blind number; and since he wasn't in the city directory either, how was I going to locate him in time to polish off the Eberfeldt bumpery mess and get myself out of the grease?

Abruptly an idea spanked me on the chops. "Sonya Levinska!" I whispered to myself with considerable excitement; whereupon I blipped back outdoors to my rambling wreck, tromped some speed out of it and headed for the Miracle Mile district on Wilshire.

Presently I dragged anchor in front of a bungalow court on a side street, barged toward the rearmost cottage and thumbed the bell button. In a

moment the portal opened and I was confronted by the queen of the Amazons in person—or at least she'd pass as an Amazon queen until a bigger one came along to dethrone her, a very remote possibility indeed.

SONYA LEVINSKA had to be seen to be believed.

She was built along the general proportions of a Diesel locomotive but twice as streamlined. I stand six feet plus in my sox and weigh a hundred and ninety on an empty stomach, and yet this Russian cookie made me look, by comparison, like a midget kneeling in a post hole. A wild curly mop of blue-black hair added another six inches to her height, which she needed the way I needed cirrhosis of the liver, and she had muscles that would have made a heavyweight wrestler yell for protection. With it all, she was perfectly proportioned; a towering Juno with the curves of a magnified Venus. Her map was equally gorgeous, the skin as white and smooth as a baby's and her profile exquisitely chiseled, like a cameo. One gander at her and you didn't know whether to be dazzled by her beauty or stunned insensible by her size.

I'd known Sonya a long time; was hep to her career and her Hollywood history. She'd emigrated to this country from Minsk or Omsk or some such outlandish region, and at one time or another she'd been variously a circus side-show strong woman, a waitress, a studio extra, a specialty dancer in a Main Street burleycue house, a shill for gambling joints and a riveter in a boiler factory that made army tanks during the war. Moreover, she had been a huge success in all these occupations—except for one minor failing. The bottle.

She was partially plastered now. I could tell it the

instant I lamped her loose kisser, the muddiness of her dark brown glims. She was wearing a set of white silk lounging pajamas that looked absolutely spectacular on her, and she was swaying slightly on her pins, trying to keep her balance.

She wasn't too boiled to recognize me, though. She blinked at me foggily and let out a throaty thunderous roar of welcome. "Iss my old palsy-walsy Sheer-luck!"

"Sherlock," I corrected her.

"That's what I have been saying. Sneerlick. Coming on insides, snoopsy-woopsy. Gives it right away a slug of wodka. You liking wodka, hah?"

I preferred Scotch but I didn't mention it; she might have been offended and torn off one of my arms, beaten me over the dandruff with it. "I love vodka," I lied, stepping inside her modest stash. "Trot out the jug and we'll irrigate."

She moved erratically to a cellarette, brought forth two tumblers and a sealed bottle with a Soviet label. Then, searching for a corkscrew but not finding one, she took the neck of the bottle between the forefinger and thumb of her left hand and pinched it. There was a crunching of glass as the neck collapsed. She tossed the fragments aside, along with the cork. "Iss very fragile material they using these days," she remarked. "In old times I having to do that with my right band."

"Ever get cut?" I said politely.

She waved a massive fist at me. "Iss taking more than pieces of glass to hurt Sonya. Callouses I getting from bucking a riveter gun, iss not denting my skin even with a razor. You thinking Russians are being softies, hah, fleetfoot?"

"Flatfoot."

"Yah. Leave us having a drinks woks." She poured the two tumblers full to the brim, handed me one, tilted the other to her avid yap and drained it with one swift gulp. I took a sip of mine and damned near died. It was like having an atom bomb going down your gullet by jet propulsion and exploding before it hit bottom. Smoke spurted out of my ears, tears sprang into my peepers and I felt my shoestrings coming untied.

"Good!" I said weakly.

"Good stuff, hah, snoopsy?"

"Oh, excellent," I moaned. "Got to have a chaser, though."

I STAGGERED blindly to the kitchen, turned on the cold-water spigot and held my face under it until the flames went out. Then I poured the rest of my vodka down the drain, whereupon there was a sizzling sound as the pipes dissolved. That plumbing would never be the same again.

Sonya leered at me from the doorway. "So you couldn't tooking it."

"Sure I can, only right now I've got to stay sober."

"Iss being something the matters with you, huh? Maybe you are getting an invalid?" She was suddenly concerned.

I said: "Oh, no, nothing like that. My health is perfect, barring the blisters I just raised in my throat. I think I could harvest them and sell them for watermelons."

"What you needing is a drinks wodka."

"Ix-nay. What I need is information. When did you start working for Flash Baudello?"

She grinned, displaying a mouthful of gorgeously white crockery. "Now iss coming out the reason for you wisiting Sonya. I have thinking it iss something like that. I noticing you in the audience last week at that stag smokering when I am do muscle dance in a jeeze string and bending horse-shoes with my toes. You enjoying Sonya's act, hah, Fido?"

"Philo," I said. "Yeah, I enjoyed it fine."

"Iss nice. Iss good to having somebody appreciating my artistical stoff. Sonya giff you a hug for speaking sweetly words." She grabbed me before I could defend myself, wrapped her arms around me and squeezed. That crackling sound was my bones giving way under the strain, and I'm afraid I groaned a little. She turned me loose, regarded me gravely and said: "Somethings is being wrong with you, glumscrew?"

"Gumshoe," I whispered faintly.

"Do not be repeating everything I saying. Iss asking you the question. Somethings is being wrong with you? You sickly or somethings?"

I said: "Not at all. I wasn't using those ribs anyhow. No, I feel grand, except the police are after me."

"What for they are being after you, hah?"

"For murder."

"Who you have been killing, hey? Tell Sonya."

"I haven't killed anybody. All I'm trying to do is collar the guilty party—and you can help me."

She looked pleased. "Iss being glad. You telling me who iss it and I tearing him apart to pieces. Like this." She picked up a phone book and casually ripped it in half. "That iss how I taking care of anybodies which putting a palsy-walsy of mine in the corners pocketing."

"You don't have to go that far," I assured her fervently. "I just thought maybe since you've started working in stag shows for Flash Baudello that you could give me his address."

"Baudello, huh? He iss being in a jam, I'm hope?"

"More or less," I said. "You see, a former vice-squad copper entitled Percival Eberfeldt got croaked this evening, and—"

She leaped for the vodka bottle. "Eberfeldt is being a corpse? Hooray. I drinking a toots!"

"Toast."

"Toast, toots, iss the same difference. You drinking a toast, you going on a toots. See what I meaning? Here, have a slugs wodka. We will celbrating Eberfeldt is being dead."

I waved away the bottle, so she poured some down her own gullet straight from the crushed neck. I watched her, waiting for her to fall down. When she didn't I said: "What makes you so happy Eberfeldt got chilled? Did you know him?"

"You being damned right. If ever there iss a stinkerish, no-good guys, was that lousy Eberfeldt. Shakings down he iss putting on girls which dancing kootchie. Shakings down he iss also putting on Flash Baudello which iss hiring girls to dancing kootchie. Playing both middles against the end iss this Eberfeldt, because he iss collect from the performers and he iss collecting from the producer. See what I meaning?"

"Yeah."

She made an enraged gesture. "Not only thiss, but no-good Baudello iss hold back a percentage from our wages by claiming he iss have to paying protection to Eberfeldt. So kootchie dancers iss paying twice. All but me," she added significantly. "I saying to both of them when they trying to put the biting on me, I saying I am smashing in somebody's heads if they don't laying off. And I'm make it stick, too."

That was all very interesting, especially the part about smashing heads. All you had to do was look at her and you knew she was just the jane who could do it. Meanwhile, though, I had other matters on my mind. "Look, hon," I said. "The important thing right now is Baudello's home address. That's what I came here for. Can you give it to me?"

"You betting." And she mentioned a number over on Hillcrest.

I thanked her, blew her a kiss and scrammed for the great outdoors, followed by her plaintive roar to the effect that I'd forgotten to join her in a stirrup cup of vodka. Ignoring this, I arrowed toward my jalopy; at which juncture a voice growled out of the darkness: "Freeze, wise guy. But fast."

It was Dave Donaldson, with a bruise on his wattles and a service .38 in his duke. He looked meaner than rat poison.

## CHAPTER VI
*Very Pretty Payoff*

I CHOKED: "How the hell did you get here?"

"I put your car license on the short wave," he answered grimly. "I had every cop in town on the lookout for it. Sure enough, a motorbike man spotted your tags parked in front of this court and flashed me the good news; so I drove right over. A wonderful invention, radio. And now I'm taking you to the can," he added in a menacing tone. "I'll teach you not to hit me when my guard is down, you double-crossing creep!"

I drew a resigned sigh and winced as the air hit

my splintered ribs. "Okay, let's drift. But don't expect any more help from me on the Eberfeldt kill."

"Any *more* help from you?" he yodeled resentfully. "What the hell help have I got from you thus far?"

"Plenty, even though you don't know it."

He leered. "I've got you. That's enough for me."

"Yeah, but I'm not the murderer."

"Ah. I suppose it was Santa Claus."

"Flash Baudello might lay odds against that," I said.

"Baudello again! Say, wait a minute. Have you located him by any remote chance? I've had the net out for him on a pickup-for-questioning but we can't even find out where he lives."

"You didn't ask the right people," I said. "Thereby saving yourself a blistered tonsil and some cracked slats."

He didn't get what I meant. "Stow the double-talk, Hawkshaw. Do you or don't you know where to find Baudello?"

"I do."

He yeeped: "Then what the damnation hell are we waiting for? Come on!" And he boosted me into his official chariot, slid in under the wheel beside me, heeled the starter button and poured a charge of ethyl into his cylinders. We took off.

I jockeyed him to Hillcrest, told him the number of the Baudello igloo. It turned out to be a counter-

feit Moorish drop with a lot of rococo stucco orna-
mentation, just the brand of blatant architecture that
would appeal to a lug like Baudello. Donaldson
clamped down on his brakes. "Remember, snoop, as
far as I'm concerned you're still under the gun. I'm
making this call just to keep the record clear, savvy?"

"Skip it," I snarled. "I'm about to hand you the
murderer if my intuition hasn't stripped a gear."
Then I raced for Baudello's portico and tried the
front doorknob.

It didn't yield. Dave said: "Now what?"

"This," I growled, fishing out my ring of master
keys. After four tries I found one that worked. Then
I blipped inside, Dave breathing down my neck as
he followed.

There was a light in one of the rooms to our left.
And voices were babbling there: a man's whining
bleat and a dame's sinister mutter. The guy was pro-
testing wildly: "You can't do this, kiddo. You can't
get away with it."

"I can try. At least you won't be alive to tell what
you saw in Eberfeldt's apartment this evening."

"But I didn't see you, baby. I swear I didn't! All I
did was go there and open the door. The room was
dark. I used my pocket flashlight and took a look at
Eberfeldt; realized he was dead when he didn't blink
in the glare. Then I beat it. I didn't see you in the
room, honest I didn't. I wouldn't have known it,
ever, if you hadn't come here just now and told

me—"

"It's no use, Flash. I'm going to kill you. I've got to."

That was my cue. I went surging through the doorway; drew out my gat and caterwauled: *"Okay, Barbara Elliot, your goose is cooked to a complete crisp!"*

THE CUDDLESOME blonde muffin whirled, lamped me and sagged until it seemed that all her plump curves were deflated in her garish red satin dress. She went pasty under her heavy makeup; dropped the roscoe which she had been aiming at Flash Baudello's ellybay. "Y-you—!" she whispered.

I said: "In person, babe. And I'm putting the finger on you for croaking Eberfeldt in his flat tonight. Also for attempting to cool Baudello, here, so he couldn't stool on you."

"You . . . you heard?"

"Plenty." I nodded. "Enough to prove my hunch was right that you're the killer." I steadied my gat at her.

"How did you g-guess?" she gasped.

"It cuts back to the first time I met you in your own wigwam on Nichols Canyon Road. Your sister Sally invited you to kick my teeth out, remember? Well, it seemed to me I'd seen you somewhere before—although I couldn't quite tab you at the time."

She just stared at me, her glims panicky.

I went on: "Well, later, when you and Sally were

brought into Eberfeldt's apartment and denied knowing me, I finally placed you. Your extra-heavy makeup and that sophisticated frock you're wearing triggered my memory. I remembered you as one of the dolls who did kootch dances at a certain stag smoker I had attended recently. You worked for Flash Baudello."

Her tongue darted out nervously, licked at dry lips. "How did you figure that c-connected me with Eberfeldt's in-murder?"

"It gave me a springboard," I said. "Eberfeldt's bank book indicated graft, shakedown, blackmail. And yet, according to your original story, he had clipped you for dough, a check and jewelry to the tune of five yards—and had actually given you a receipt with my name signed to it. Now why would he pull such a screwball stunt as forging my moniker? As cagy and smart as he was—and he had to be smart to make a living the way he made his—it seemed to me that he wouldn't have pulled anything as raw as that. I mean the whole story fell apart when I tried to match it up with Eberfeldt's character."

"But . . . but—"

"So it began to look as if maybe you'd lied about your afternoon's experience. Perhaps you hadn't met the guy in a cocktail dispensary. Maybe you hadn't got drunk at all. Possibly you had known Eberfeldt quite a while; and instead of going to his flat to get sobered up, perhaps you'd gone there for another reason entirely."

"Such as?" Her voice was weak, quavery with apprehension.

I said: "To make a payoff. Eberfeldt was a con man, a gyp artist, a blackmailer; maybe he was blackmailing you. You'd be a logical victim for his operations; after all, you were leading a double life. To your sister you were an innocent young chick, inexperienced and naive. But actually you were performing in some of Baudello's stag shows. Don't deny it, because I saw you myself only a few nights ago."

"I . . . I'm not denying it," she said dully.

"Yeah. So assume Eberfeldt was shaking you down the way he did a lot of other janes. Okay; you visited him this afternoon to pay him the usual hush money, and he boosted the bite much higher."

"That's exactly wh-what he did. And I couldn't stand it. . . ." Her voice trailed off.

I nodded. "So on the spur of the moment you picked up something heavy and conked him, killed him. Then, realizing what you'd done, you knew you were in a jackpot. And like most amateurs in homicide you tried to dope out some way of keeping in the clear, finding a fall guy to take the rap. Hell, if you had just walked out of his flat and left his body there, the chances are you would never have been linked to it. But no; you had to embroider the scenario. And you thought of me."

"I w-wish I hadn't."

I SAID THEN: "It's too late for regrets, kitten. The point is, you had heard of my reputation as a quick-trigger man, which made me a likely prospect for the frame you were scheming. You faked a phony story to tell your sister, and backed that story up with a ridiculous receipt which you forged yourself, using my name on the bottom of it. Superficially it was a clever gag. Sally fell for it; dragged me into the mess—just as you hoped she would."

"You know everyting, don't you?" she said bitterly.

I shrugged. "Practically everything. You figured I would head for Eberfelt's flat and demand a show-down with him. I didn't realize he was dead all the time—but you knew it because you had killed him. Okay. You sneaked to his apartment ahead of me; waited for me to arrive. Then bad luck tossed a monkey wrench into your plot. Flash Baudello showed up to make a payoff. He used his pocket flash, piped Eberfeldt's remnants and got scared sweatless. He took a fast powder."

"And?"

"Right after that, I ankled in. *You fired a blank cartridge at me.* That explains why the cops didn't find any bullet in the wall, later. At the time, however, I didn't know it was a blank. Naturally I thought somebody was trying to plug me; so I shot back twice in self-defense. I put two pills in Eberfeldt's corpse. Then you sneaked up on me in the darkness, bopped me unconscious and lit a shuck for home."

Her kisser twisted in a wry grimace. "I've m-made a mess of everything, haven't I? Including my own life."

"Looks that way, hon. Because after I had doped it all out, I set a trap for you. When the cops brought you to corroborate my story and you denied knowing me, I deliberately planted a scare in your mind. I hinted that maybe Baudello had tabbed the murderer in Eberfeldt's apartment."

"*Now* you tell me!" She laughed harshly.

I nodded. "If you were as guilty as 1 suspected, I knew you'd go on a hunt for Baudello and try to shut him up, permanently. He was a menace to you as long as he stayed alive—you thought. However, since you were a dancer on his payroll, you were bound to know his home address."

"So?"

"I counted on the cops detaining you just long enough for me to find out where he lived. It took me a blistered gullet and some cracked ribs to get that information from an oversized Russian muffin named Sonya Levinska, but I finally made the grade. Then I rammed into Lieutenant Donaldson and we both got here to Baudello's joint in time to keep you from pulling another kill."

She turned, walked slowly toward Dave with her wrists extended. "I'm ready to go to prison. But please don't drag Sally into it. She had nothing to do with . . . anything that happened she doesn't even suspect that I've been a . . . a—"

"Kootch dancer?" Dave supplied politely "Hell, girlie, that's nothing to be ashamed of. Keep your chin up. After all, Eberfeldt was a louse and got what he deserved. Maybe the jury will give you a break—if Turner doesn't press charges for the frame you tried to pin on him. And if Baudello, here, keeps quiet about the way you almost bumped him off. . . ."

For once in his life Donaldson called the turn. The jury did give Barbara a break. Instead of putting her into the gas chamber they merely sent her to the bastile for the rest of her natural life.

# TO THE READER

---

If you enjoyed this book, you will be glad to know that there are many others just as well written, just as interesting, to be had in the Fiction House Press Library.

You will find the Fiction House Press Library online at

www.FictionHousePress.com

Made in the USA
Middletown, DE
03 July 2022

68388626R00149